In the Name of Queen

A novel by

Sateesh Patil

Prologue

The second stop of the morning

That's where she boarded the train.

Already the flustered state was settling in on the young man's nerves as he glanced up from his book, peeping over the edges of the pages. He was attempting to look discreet, but the woman looked up from the inside of her bag that she was rummaging through. She probably would have been frightened. However, for the time being, the man named Jane was safe as he watched her take the seat.

As usual, she was on her cell phone, a frustrated look on her face as she spoke to whoever was on the line. There was a folder that she pulled out from her bag as she flipped through several pieces of paper, her hands shaking to the point where she nearly dropped the folder twice within the span of thirty seconds.

He watched her as she rubbed her forehead until her skin turned an irritable red before she began biting her nails, a nervous habit of hers that he had witnessed on numerous occasions, especially when she was on her cell phone.

"R-right! I'll have those papers to you as soon as I arrive. I promise. " She stammered. She waited for a moment for the person to respond until she pulled the cell phone away from her ear with a confused look. "Hello?" "Mr. Daniel?"

Leaving out a heavy sigh, loud enough for Jane to hear, she dropped her phone into her lap and turned to look out the window. While she faced away from others on the train, her reflection was clear in the glass, allowing Jane to catch a glimpse of the sole tear that had escaped before she quickly wiped it away.

At that moment, all Jane wanted to do was reach out to the young girl and tell her everything was going to be okay.

But he couldn't, for many reasons. You can guess that.

For one, he wasn't bold enough to approach a being of such beauty, or any stranger for that matter. Not like the countless men that had done so in the past as they approached her with their charming grins and smooth words. No, his lack of confidence has caused him to keep Jane to himself, observing her from behind a book.

During his time of observing her, he was able to witness many things about her that made his heart race in his chest. Like her laugh, one of his most favourite sounds, because it was so rare to hear. Not many things made her laugh, but Jane welcomed anything that could.

However, while he was able to witness the good, he also noticed the bad. Like how she had dropped a drastic number of pounds since the first time he saw her board the train. She looked so fragile, he was afraid if she fell, her body would shatter as if her bones were made of glass. She had been slender to begin with, but now her shoulder blades struck out through the back of her shirt. It didn't help that her clothing was made of a thin material that made her figure stick out even more.

Neha

Neha Raj was her name.

Atleast, that was the name she said when she answered her phone. That was the name of the woman that Jane couldn't stop thinking about when he stepped off the train. She was the woman that made him smile, even though they didn't talk. Jane's morning was sort of made by seeing her in the morning. Her voice, while timid on the phone, was always so cool that he would even get cold fever.

Why has she had this effect on him? He had no idea. They hadn't even exchanged a greeting with each other. To his recollection, he was fairly certain that Neha didn't even know that they rode the same train every morning. But there was Jane, ready to accept her flaws and all. He wanted to make her laugh, tell whoever Mr. Daniel was to go to hell for making her upset in the mornings, and make her hearty meals every chance he got so that he knew that she was eating well.

Jane peered over his book again, this time to see Neha rummaging through her bag, most likely for her Suduko book, which she had just finished.He smiled to himself because the number puzzles always seemed to irritate her, and he could always hear her muttering curses under her breath as she erased countless times.

He wanted to ask her why she bothered with the puzzle if all it ever did was make her angry.

He wanted to ask her how her day was.

He wanted to ask her out to coffee or perhaps dinner, to be honest.

He just wanted to say something to her.

even if it was just a hello.

Jane talks to him.

"Go, Jane, go," he said, after his setting the book in the empty seat beside him as he turned his body to face her seat.

It's just a simple hello. You can do it. It's a five-letter word. two syllables. Hello, Or even HI. It is only a two-letter word, one syllable. Hi,

Lifting his hand, he practised his wave a couple of times to himself until he realised how crazy he probably looked to the other passengers on the train. His face flushed before he ran his sweaty palms over the top of his trousers.

The train was beginning to slow down and the familiar scenery as they came around to the station came to an eventual halt. He cleared his throat, adjusted his tie, and prayed that he didn't screw up.

Standing up, he approached the seat where Neha was and opened his mouth, ready to speak.

"H..."

When the doors to the train opened, he suddenly lost all ability to speak as Neha stood up and collected her belongings.

He froze in place and just watched as Neha didn't even look over her shoulder at him before she left her seat and walked off the train, leaving Jane alone.

Another opportunity missed.

Jane cleared his throat before shifting back and forth awkwardly on his feet.

"Hi.....!"

1

Neha Raj

Neha, darling, it's your mother... again. I haven't heard from you or your sister today. I was just checking to see if you two were alright. Also, I wanted to talk about you and Sasha coming for a bit of brunch on Sunday. Anyhow, I'll ring call your sister again and see if she answers. It's-"

Neha Raj drew her arm back into the tub as her cell phone began playing through all the voicemails she had missed throughout the day. Some by accident, others on purpose.

Neha, it's Arjun. Again, please just answer the phone or my text. Or something. We need to talk.

"No, we don't," the girl replied, pressing the button to delete the voice mail.

"There are no more messages."

The young brunette submerged herself under the water completely, with the exception of her nose and eyes. After a long day at work dealing with her monstrous boss, all Neha wanted to do was relax in peace and quiet. She had the perfect opportunity to do so, as her apartment was completely silent that afternoon. The relaxing scent of lavender, along with being surrounded by luscious bubbles in her tub, she was all set to spend a couple of hours, but the world had different plans for Ms. Neha when she received an obnoxiously loud knock on the bathroom door.

She thought about keeping quiet and pretending that she wasn't home, but her elder sister was not one to be easily fooled.

"Neha, are you decent?" Sasha's voice rang out after a couple of more knocks on the door.

"I'm in the tub," Neha replied, with an eye roll.

"What do you think?"

"Well, can you cover up so I can come in?"

"Can't you wait until after I'm finished?" Neha called back.

I'm trying to take a bath, and I know this sounds crazy, but I would love a few moments to myself without interruption.

"I have to leave for my shift in a few minutes," Shasta informed her. "Come on, I'll only be a minute."

"For hell's sake, Sasha," Neha sighed quietly as she pushed herself out of the tub and grabbed her towel. Once it was wrapped around her body, she allowed her sister to come in as she sat down on the edge of the tub.

"Are you okay?" her elder sister asked, a wave of concern washing over her face as she spotted Neha shivering. However, it wasn't due to the fact that she was feeling ill, but more along the lines that she had left a stream bath and was surrounded by the cold air of the room.

"Despite the fact that my bath has been interrupted, yes, I feel fine."

"I'm going to be working late this evening." Sasha continued to draw her mousy brown hair back into a ponytail. So if you should need anything, I'll have the ringer on my phone up and I already spoke with Mr. Girish."

"Sister, you didn't have to talk to Mr. Girish. I told you I'm fine."

The last thing she wanted was for their elderly neighbour to be dragged into matters. Whenever Neha had to be left alone, Sasha made sure to contact someone to come check on Neha as if she was a kid that had to be let out to tinkle or needed attention before she got lonely.

"You seem awfully stressed lately, Neha," Sasha said, walking over and sitting next to her on the tub edge. "I just have to be sure that you'll be alright when I am not around."

"I will be. I can normally tell when they're coming on. It's not like I'm taking this medicine for nothing. If I feel like one is heading my way, I'll gladly go to Mr. Girish. Does that make you feel better? "

"A little." Look, if you need anything, do not hesitate to ask. Just call me; you know I'll answer for you. "

Neha didn't want to discuss her medical condition anymore. She really just wanted to be left alone. "Can I return to my bath now?"

"Yes, but don't stay in there too long, you'll start to look like Nana."

Neha snorted. "Bye sister."

After she heard the front door to the apartment closed over and the top lock rattle with Sasha locking it, Neha dropped her towel and climbed back into the water, which, to her luck, was still incredibly warm. She closed her eyes as she rested her head back and tried to settle her mind again.

Her sister had been right. Of course, she was stressed out, but it wasn't just from work, it was also due to everyone being all over her since the accident.

Having a grand mal seizure behind the wheel of her car didn't only frighten Neha but everyone in her family. She was lucky to walk away from the crash without any serious injuries, but mentally, Neha was scarred from the wreck.

The usual signs of her seizures hadn't come to give her a warning, or she would have pulled over. She hadn't suffered from one in so long due to her medication that she had been completely off guard. a numbness. Only to wake up to the sounds of sirens and an emergency crew trying to help her regain consciousness.

Her car was completely totaled, wrapped around the base of a tree. Both the tree and Neha survived, though, and no one else was hurt. except for Neha. She didn't want to get behind the wheel of a car ever again with the fear of suffering another seizure and the chance of not being so lucky a second time. It wasn't a hard task, but she no longer has her licence as her doctor wouldn't clear her. To get it previously, she had to go a year on her previous medication without having a seizure. It didn't seem like a big accomplishment to gain her freedom and independence from her family. It was a huge step. But it was all lost in a matter of minutes in an accident.

After a week of being driven to work by Sasha, Neha couldn't take it. The constant questions of if she was alright or how she was feeling every second of the ride was enough to drive her crazy. It was then that she decided to take the train to work.

Her mother begged her to allow Sasha to continue driving her. However, Neha hated being dependent on someone all the time. She hated watching her sister reschedule things or cancel going somewhere in order to watch over her. It made Neha feel like a burden.

All Neha wanted to do was live a normal life without the seizures interrupting her at the most inconvenient times.

Neha was diagnosed with epilepsy at the age of eight. She had a hard time remembering what life was like without worrying about the seizures.

Her medication helped drastically. When she was younger, she was prone to having a seizure a couple of times a day, but slowly the seizures began to span out in time. Sometimes Neha could go months without one, and everything seemed fine until it occurred and ruined everything. But lately, after the accident, her seizures were becoming a bit more frequent despite the medication.

A bunch of weight she didn't need to lose.

During the mornings when she was getting ready for work, she avoided the mirror at all costs. The mirror only reminded her of how sick she really looked, and it was obvious when her family and friends were worried about her. Her condition hadn't only put a strain on the relationship between her and her family, but her love life had taken quite a hit as well.

Her friend of a year, Arjun, decided that Neha and her seizures were just too overwhelming for him. He broke up with her one evening after telling her that he was just so stressed out and needed to focus on himself. He used the excuse of how he needed to make himself happy before he could make her happy.

Of course, only a couple of days later did he come crawling back, begging Neha to take him back into her life, but she refused. Besides her family, Neha decided it would be best to just keep herself to herself for most of the time. She didn't bother to make new friends or reach out to anyone in fear that they would abandon her just as Arjun did. Her epilepsy would more than likely be lifelong, and if people couldn't understand that, she didn't want them to get involved.

She wanted someone to understand.

She wanted someone who didn't see her as a burden.

She grabbed a shirt and sweatpants, throwing them on when there was a knock on the door. Neha sighed, knowing who it was. She walked to the front door and opened it to find Mr. Girish, their neighbour, standing outside.

"Hello Neha!" the old man greeted her, lifting his cap slightly, revealing the few silver strands of his hair that were struggling to remain.

"Hello, Mr. Girish." She smiled kindly.

I hope I wasn't disturbing you. I just wanted to let you know that I was running to the store for a few minutes, just in case you needed me for anything. "

"Oh, don't worry, I'm fine."

Neha hated that the most, how everyone believed she couldn't be alone for more than a few minutes without having a seizure and dying right then and there. She was angry, not at the man; she knew he was only doing what was asked for, but angry with herself for letting it get so bad. For letting her family become so paranoid and worried about her that she was forced to live such a life.

"Take your time," she told him. "I'll just be lying on the sofa watching some news."

"Alright, I promise I won't be long. I'll run around the store if I have to. "

"That really isn't..." she didn't get to finish as the man trotted off.

Neha rested her head on a throw pillow and stared blankly at the news anchor who was rambling on and on about something having to do with foreign affairs. She rolled onto her back and stared up at the ceiling.

If anyone is up there and listening, I don't know if I did anything in a past life to deserve all this. I must have done something awful, even though I'm not sure what. But if that's the case, I'm sorry for whatever I did. Perhaps apologies won't cut it, but can I at least catch a break? I'd really appreciate it. "

2

Jane Maya

He had choked.

He choked again.

He had been so close to finally talking to her and failed.

All Jane wanted to do when he stepped off the train was to kick himself repeatedly. Even hours after it happened, he was still tearing up about it as he arrived home to his apartment. He flung himself back on his sofa, rubbing his face with both hands, letting out frustrated noises in between his own scoldings.

"What is wrong with you, Jane? Why can't you just talk to her? You talk to people every day; it's part of your job, and yet you can't say hello to this one person! " He reprimanded

"Are you talking to yourself in there again?"

Jane lifted his hands from his face and elevated his head to see his roommate, Mourya, standing in the doorway of the hall watching him with a bowl of popcorn in hand, munching away a handful as he waited for an answer.

"Yes," Jane answered. "Yes, I am."

"Why? What's wrong? Is it that girl again? " Mourya walked in further and took a place in an empty armchair. Jane sat up to face him with an exasperated look in his eyes.

I came this close to talking to her! ' Jane said, holding his thumb and index finger slightly apart for emphasis.

"This is close and I..."

"Choked?"

"I choked."

"Dude, how hard is it to just say hello to someone? I mean, am I supposed to be offended or something? So you do not see me as a person? Is that why it's so easy for you to say hello to me? " He let out a dramatic sobbing noise, but it quickly ended as he nearly dropped his popcorn. The man made a grab for the bowl and held it as if it were his first newborn.

"It isn't hard," Jane began, "I know that. but it just happens around her for some reason. "

"She either has to be the most beautiful or most intimidating girl out there to cause this much anxiety in you." I haven't seen you so worked up over something or someone since you had to go to the principal's office when we were kids. And you weren't even the one in trouble at the time. I was. "

"I can't help it." Jane sighed, taking one of the sofa pillows and placing it over his face. She just has that effect on me. Everything about her is just... amazing.

And I just want to open my mouth and ask her if she would like to get a cup of coffee, but every single time I try... nothing comes out. It's like she has some weird superpower that keeps me from approaching her. No matter how hard I try, she manages to render me speechless. "

Mourya shook his head with a roll of his eyes. You're madly in love with this girl, and yet you haven't even uttered a greeting. Do you see where the problem lies in that, Jane? "

Jane ripped the pillow away. "Of course I do. Do you think I like stammering like a fool in her presence? I'd love to ask her out, but I can't. My tongue just swells in my mouth and I can't form words. My brain draws a blank and I can't do anything but stand there and stare. "

"Then grow a pair and sit next to the woman and strike up a conversation, Jane."

"You make it sound so easy, but it's not, Mourya, and you know this!"

"Look buddy, I'm just trying to help you out there, because if you go through life like this, I'm afraid it's going to be quite a sad journey to the end."

Jane glanced over at Mourya, who was looking at him with sincerity in his eyes.

"And if you really can't find your voice, bring it back to school times and write the woman a note. Pretend you're mute or dumb or something," Mourya shrugged.

"Write her a note?"

Yeah, scribble something down, even if it's just the word "hi." At least it'll get you somewhere. "

"You think so?"

"Yes, now, tomorrow, hand her the note and see where it goes."

"What if she doesn't read it?"

"Then don't bother with her anymore." Plain and simple? "

Jane frowned. It was easy for Mourya to say that. He didn't see her. He didn't know the things that Jane did about Neha. To Mourya, Neha was just another broad of sagging potential, but he would never have waited on a girl so long. He would just move on to the next woman that caught his eye. But that was the last thing on Jane's mind.

"Alright, I'll write her a note. I'll do it! " Jane said in a determined voice as he jumped to his feet.

"That's the spirit! Feeling a little better? "

"Yea, actually."

"Good, good," Mourya said before standing up from his chair. "Now get off the sofa, the games are about to start and you're in my spot."

A surge of confidence raced through Jane's veins as he stood up, thinking about the note he would hand to the girl the next morning.

He wouldn't fail this time.

The train was running late that morning. Jane knew it would add to Neha's stressful state, as it always did when it ran behind schedule. Normally, it was because Mr. Daniel would give her hell about her tardiness. No matter how many times she tried to explain it over the phone, it didn't seem to change anything. It would only end with Mr. Daniel hanging up on her and Neha sitting through the rest of the train ride with a miserable look on her face. He checked his watch over and over. He didn't want to approach her if she was upset. It didn't really look good on his behalf, but then he thought, maybe it would cheer her up to have someone to talk to.

When the train came to its second stop, there she was, a frown prominent on her face, but no phone to her ear. He could only assume the phone call had already taken place between her and Mr. Daniel. She walked onto the train and took her usual spot, avoiding any eye contact with fellow passengers. Although occasionally, he could see her lifting the sleeve of her shirt to her eyes to wipe the tears away, leaving her shirt stained with the droplets of water.

Jane set his book beside him and wiped his palms onto his slacks as he dug into his things to pull a piece of paper and then removed the pen from his pocket. He set the tip of the pen to the paper and began to debate what to write.

Should he just write a simple hello or perhaps ask her how she was doing? Should he write down her name?

No, he thought quickly. There was no doubt in his mind that she would probably find that creepy. She hadn't formally introduced herself to the passengers on the train, and she would probably wonder how he knew it.

He placed the pen down and sighed. He even choked while writing a note to her. He figured he should have just written it before she boarded the train. Now he was finding himself all sorts of flustered.

Biting the inside of his cheek, Jane looked up from his lap to look at Neha.

But she wasn't there anymore.

His eyebrows knitted in confusion immediately as he turned his head to look around. He scanned the train. Where had she gone?

Suddenly, a screech brought his attention back to the front. A woman passenger was pointing to the ground with a panicked look on her face just as Jane stood up to see Neha on the ground.

Wasting no time, he leaped over his seat and made his way to Neha's side as she was lying there. Her body was stiff as her muscles moved her in an uncomfortable jerking motion. She had a nasty gash on her head from where she had fallen.

Jane was panicking, but he couldn't waste any time. He saw the saliva building up in her mouth along with some blood as it appeared she might have bitten her tongue or hit her mouth when she fell. The gurgling sounds from her throat echoed through the train as she lost the ability to swallow. Kneeling down, Jane quickly turned the woman on her side to allow the pool of spit to drain from her mouth. He turned to look over his shoulder at the other passengers that were standing around unsure of what to do. He told one man to call for help. They were close to the station; they could help her there.

"What's happening?" someone asked.

"I-I think she's having a seizure..." Jane said, even though he wasn't sure. He had gone from being medically qualified to taking a first aid course a few years ago and never thinking about it again.

His hands were shaking as he placed them on Neha. Her jerking began to subside, but the wound on her head was still bleeding.

"Here!" a woman offered some napkins to him.

"Thanks." He grabbed the napkins and placed them on Neha's forehead in hopes of stopping the blood flow.

3

The Note

Whispers

All Neha could hear when she finally regained her full consciousness was a load of whispers. The girl opened her eyes, slowly adjusting to the light to find herself surrounded by strangers. All of them looked extremely concerned. She automatically assumed what happened. She could feel the soreness of her muscles, but her head was aching fiercely. The awful taste of blood lingered in her mouth as her tongue throbbed in her mouth.

She went to lift her hand to the part of her forehead that hurt the most, but a parademic quickly intercepted.

"You've got quite a nasty gash up there, I suggest not touching it," the man said. Neha attempted to sit up while everyone stared at her. She went to use both hands when she felt something in her right hand.

A piece of paper was folded up in her palm, and while her memory normally wasn't the greatest after one of her seizures, she surely didn't remember writing a note earlier.

"Miss, we are going to bring you to the hospital so we can get your head checked out and call someone to pick you up," the paramedic told her. "Do you feel any sort of dizziness?"

"No."

"Besides the pain from the cut on your forehead, do you feel any other head pain?"

"I don't know." I can't differentiate right now. My head hurts, yes. She squinted from the powerful throbbing coming from her forehead.

"Alright, well let's get you situated."

Neha brushes off the man's words before looking at the note in her hand.

"The gentleman who helped you left," an observing woman told her with a smile.

Neha glanced over at her. "What?"

"The man who helped you when you fell and went unconscious on the train." He left that paper in your hand and then left in an awful hurry. "

While the paramedics were placing her on the ambulance, Neha tucked the note into her pocket and allowed them to take her away.

"Oh Neha!"

Neha cringed at Sasha's high-pitched squeal as the woman ran into the room. She had been situated in a room after her vitals had been monitored by the nurse and doctor. Her gaze had been focused on the small television, and she had just been about to drift off when her sister's voice echoed loudly in the hospital room.

"Hey, Sasha." Neha greeted her with far less enthusiasm as she pushed herself to sit up in bed.

"Are you okay?" Sasha immediately made her way to Neha's bedside and sat down. Oh, look at your head! What happened? "

With her older sister on the verge of tears and making an absolute scene inside the hospital room, Neha just wanted to disappear or vanish into a dark hole for eternity.

"I'm fine, Sasha. I just bumped my head on the way down is all. "

"You had a seizure on the train, Neha."

"I also had utpa for breakfast," Neha replied in irritation.

This is no time to be kidding around. "Your Mom was right; you should let me take you to work."

"No," Neha said, shaking her head.I can manage on my own. "

"And by managing on your own, you mean to wind up in the hospital?"

"Did you come here to belittle me?"

"No, I came to see if you were alright."

We have established that I'm fine. You can go now. " Neha folded her arms across her chest and looked away from the woman.

"I'm not leaving you here alone." The doctor said they wanted to keep you overnight just in case.

Neha pulled at her hair, falling back into her pillow with a groan. She hated staying in hospitals; she hated everything about it.

I brought an overnight bag. I'll be staying with you so we can leave together in the morning. Then we can talk about me driving you to work from now on. "

It's not going to happen, Sasha. "The train is the one time where I can be alone without everyone monitoring me."

"Monitoring you? Is that what you call it? "

"What do you want to call it then?"

"How about an older sister showing her younger sister some compassion and worry over her condition?"

"You mean pity?"

I don't pity you, Neha. You know damn well that I don't pity you, but I worry about you. I'll admit that. You want to do all things, but you can't. "

"Who says?" Neha replied. "Who says that I can't do things independently?"

"Neha, listen to yourself. If someone isn't there to help you during one of your seizures, there can be a strong possibility of you dying by choking on your own spirit. "

"I can normally feel them coming on."

But you didn't feel this one coming on, did you? And you didn't feel the one coming on when you were driving that one time. "

Neha stared down at her hands with a blaring glare, leaving it to Sasha to bring up the accident to prove her point. It was a cheap shot and one that left Neha with every intention of ignoring her sister as it was completely uncalled for. She understood that there were things that she couldn't do, but she didn't need the constant reminders. It didn't help her to have people tell her she couldn't do things; there was no positivity around her. Her mother and sister continued to tell her that it wasn't a good idea for her to be driving, and when the accident occurred, she could just see the "I told you so" looks on their faces.

Sensing the tension between them, Sasha decided to leave the room and get some water to give Neha some time alone.

Her head continued to hurt from the headache, from the fall, and from Sasha too. The light from the sun beaming into the room only made it worse. She arose from the bed and walked over to close the shade. When she passed the chair, she saw her clothing had been swapped for a hospital gown. Neha didn't even want to see herself at the moment, knowing she probably resembled a stick wrapped in a used tissue.

Her eyes fell on the pants, and she saw the note sticking out of the pocket.

The Note

How could she forget?

She grabbed it and quickly made her way back to the bed before she was scolded by a nurse or, worse, by Sasha.

Her fingers shook slightly as she unfolded the piece of paper. She wasn't sure why she felt nervous about opening a note from a complete stranger. Perhaps it was because he had witnessed her in an embarrassing state. She said that just the material image of herself made her cringe, knowing fully what she looked like during one of her seizures.

What could he have possibly had to write to her?

Hello Neha,

I hope you're feeling better by the time you read this. You suffered a seizure on the train, and I did my best to make sure you didn't hurt yourself. Sorry, I couldn't catch you in time before you hit your head. I hope it doesn't hurt too badly when you wake up. I'm also sorry I couldn't stay with you the entire time. I wish I could have at least stayed until you opened your eyes. But the medics reassured me that you were going to be okay. I hope they're right.

I wish you all the best and I hope you're up and running in no time.

Queen

Jane '

Neha read it over twice before flipping the piece of paper to make sure she didn't miss anything before it settled in her lap. A small smile appeared on her face as it seemed someone had looked after her on the train, almost like a guardian angel. The pain subsided as she was distracted by how sweet the little note was, leaving her in a better mood for a short period of time.

4

The Boss

Jane ran into the office as fast as he could, his breathing short and rapid as he burst through the office doors, nearly tripping over the fraying part of the office carpet. He managed to catch himself before he fell and quickly began straightening his tie and jacket when a voice called out to him in a cold tone.

"You're late."

Jane spun around to see his boss, his eyes narrowed in Jane's direction like a hawk about to swoop down on its prey and kill him.

"I-I know, I'm so s-s-sorry, sir, but you"

"I don't want an excuse."

Jane bit his tongue as his boss held his hand up in his face. "Just get to your desk, I'll talk to you later."

"Yes, sir."

Sliding off his jacket, he threw it over the back of his chair and sat at his desk, dropping his head into his hands. The morning was off to a terrible start as he had to witness Neha suffer a seizure and wasn't even able to keep her company until she woke up. He now has to face his boss, who was a devil in human skin, and he was not going to get off easily for being late.

"Hey!" A cheery voice greeted him, causing Jane to jump and look over. His cubicle neighbour, Vishnu, popped over the wall of his desk with a bright grin. How anyone could look happy while working in hell was beyond Jane.

"Good morning, Vishnu. How are you?" He greeted him in return as he straightened himself in his chair.

"Pretty good considering I wasn't the one chewed out by the boss." Why were you so late? " The man whispered to him.

"Because the train was running late and then I got caught up in an emergency," Jane explained.

"An emergency? Are you okay? What happened? "

Vishnu was incredibly friendly in some ways, but the man lived for gossip, and when he wanted information, he could ask a million questions in the span of just a few minutes. With Jane not being a big talker at all, it was a horrible combination to have him as a cubible neighbour.

"Neh-" He began to explain, but suddenly caught himself before he revealed too much information. "Er... a girl abroad, the train suffered a seizure."

"Oh my goodness!" Vishnu clapped his hands over his mouth for a moment. "Is she alright?"

"The medics told me she was going to be okay. I figured they know best in a situation like that. "

"You didn't stick around long enough to find out?"

"I couldn't remember the boss man."

"Oh right. Yeah, he was pretty pissed when you didn't arrive on time."

"When isn't he in a foul mood? I don't control the train, and I obviously had no control over what happened on the train. Te... that girl... didn't either.But some people can't come to terms with that. It's all about being on time. "

"Time is money," Vishnu said, imitating their boss's voice.

Jane chuckled. "Don't let him hear you. Then we'll both be in trouble."

Vishnu saluted him before sinking back behind his cubible, leaving Jane to his work.

As he looked over financial reports pertaining to the firm, Jane couldn't help but think about Neha and wonder about her condition. Was she feeling alright? Did she regain consciousness?

Did she read the note he left her?

The NOTE

He had jotted it down so quickly, but as he thought back to it, Jane realised something very important. How he had signed it off.

Queen,

Jane.

" Oh Jane, you didn't." he groaned, smaking his forehead. Now, Neha would definitely believe he was sort of a creeper. Not only had he written down her name, he had signed it with the Queen and with his name.

The ringer on his desk phone went off.

"Jane—."

"My office," a voice said, and the line cut off.

Standing outside, Jane inhaled deeply before knocking on his boss's door. His hands had been trembling since he hung up the phone, and he had to work himself up to even leave his cubicle.

"Come in."

Jane turned the knob and walked in. Before he could even begin to apologize, he was being barked at like a dog.

"Sit."

He did as he was told, as if he were an obedient puppy.

"Sir I—"

His boss, Mr. Krishnan, turned around in his chair, silencing Jane with a stern look. Jane averted his gaze to the floor, submissively.

"This is the third time you've been late this quarter, Jane." And you know how I feel about tardiness."

"Yes, sir, I do. And I'm sorry, but the train-"

"If the train you are normally on is consistently late, then it is up to you to get on an earlier train and make sure you are here in this office on time."

"But the earlier train would bring me in far too early."

"That's not my problem, Jane. I will not continue to give you warnings and allow you to get away with this. The next time you're late, you're fired. I don't care if it's a minute or a second passed, you will no longer work here. Do you understand? "

"Yes, sir."

"Good, now get back to work."

"Right."

Jane rose and left the office without another word, closing the door behind him.

Working way passed the time he normally clocked out and went home, Jane rubbed his tired eyes when he heard footsteps approaching his desk. His body tensed as he already knew who was walking up on him and there was nothing he could do about it. Even Vishnu had left for the day to reassure him that everything was going to be okay.

Mr. Krishnan had a stack of files in his hands as he made his way over and set the pile on Jane's desk.

Jane clenched his jaw but said nothing.

"I expect it to be finished by the morning," Mr. Krishnan said.

"Yes, sir."

"Goodnight, Jane." His boss's voice was cold and insincere.

Jane listened to him walk away, the door opening and slamming shut, bringing him to flinch.

"Goodnight, father."

5

Pity vs Support

"What's that you got there?" Sasha asked as she returned to Neha's room with a cup of coffee and noticing the note in her sister's hand.

"Oh, nothing." Neha quickly placed her hand behind her back and tried to dismiss the idea of it, but Sasha was not about to let it go so easily.

"What the hell, what is it? You have the biggest smile on your face, so it must be something. "

There was no sense in lying to Sasha. Neha knew all too well that the woman would continue to harass her until she decided to spill the beans.

"Whoever helped me on the train... he left me a note," Neha said, handing the piece of paper to her sister.

Sasha took it carefully and scanned it over while sipping her coffee.

"Well, Queen Jane, huh?" Sasha grinned. "Sounds like you've got yourself an admirer."

"Or he was just signing it quickly, kind of like how you called that professor's mom that one day in your class." Neha giggled.

"Yeah, yeah, no one ever lets me forget that even though it happened like six years ago. I was embarrassed enough." She handed the letter back to Neha and sat in one of the chairs.

"It is sweet though. I guess he couldn't stick around until I woke up, but... it's just so sweet. I wish I could thank him personally, but..."

"But?"

"He didn't sign his last name. It just says, "Jane."

"Well, do you know Jane from the train?" Sasha asked her.

"I don't know anyone from the train. I hardly speak to anyone. I'm either on the phone with Mr. Daniel or I just stick to my suduko book."

"You're still working on those damn puzzles? I swear..."

"I just want to complete the books so I can say I completed the book with absolutely no help."

Sasha frowned. "You know, people only offer to help out of kindness, Neha. It's not always out of pity. I wish you would just accept that."

"I guess I'm just stubborn then." Neha shrugged, placing the note on her nightstand and settling back into the bed.

"So do you think that man helped you out of pity?" Sasha asked her.

"No, I think he helped me because he didn't want to see me die on the train. But that's different. I don't mind people helping me when I have a seizure, because in those moments I'm incapable of doing things. However, when I am fully aware and conscious and have people trying to get my food for me or help me with a simple number puzzle, that's what bothers me.

"But Neha, you have to come to realisation that you can't do things that everyone else does."

"And I have. I don't drive anymore, but that doesn't mean I need a chauffeur. I can manage the train. "

"You have a seizure."

"And I could have had a seizure whilst in the car with you. It happens, Sasha. This isn't new to me. I've been dealing with these for over fifteen years. And they've gotten much better, but there will be times that they will come when I least suspect it. I've come to terms with that. "

"Well, have you discussed any more options?"

"Sasha, I'm on the medication I need to be on. I've tried the diet. This is something that I'm going to live with, and the one thing I request is that people don't pity me or try to help me with everything. "

"Then what is it that you do want, Neha?"

"Support," Neha replied simply.

"Support?"

"Yes, I want my family and friends to support my decisions. If I want to take the train, rather than talk me out of it, I want you to support me. These seizures don't make you any less of an adult than you, and how would you like it if everyone always tried to talk you out of something you wanted to do?"

"I reckon I would be pissed off but-"

"But nothing, Sasha. Please, that's all I ask. No questioning, no pressuring... just support. "

"Neha, as your big sister, you know all I want to do is to support you, and so does Mom, but we're always going to worry about you. With your accident last year... Neha, we don't want to lose you. "

"And you won't. Neither of you will, alright, I'm not going anywhere. "

Sasha ended up dozing off in her chair as the two awaited for their mother to arrive that evening. Something Neha was dreading, not because she didn't like her mother, no, she loved her mother dearly. However, she knew her mother was going to make a scene the moment she arrived, especially with the lovely new gash on Neha's forehead.

With Sasha's light snoring and the machines as background noise, Neha held the note in her hands again and scanned over it, trying to remember any face outside the train. She realised how oblivious she was to all her surroundings when it came to the train. She didn't recognise any of the people that had surrounded her when she awoke, and she probably had been taking the train with them for months.

"Who are you, Jane?" she whispered. She wondered if he took the train regularly or if it was just a one-time deal, but something about his note made her think he must have been a regular among the passengers.

She was certain of one thing: she wanted to meet this Jane guy and thank him in person.

"Oh, Neha!"

Her thoughts were interrupted as her mother, as everyone affectionately called her, came barging through the door of the room. Sasha was startled awake from her peaceful slumber as their mother's loudness echoed.

"Hello, mom." Neha greeted calmly before being wrapped in a tight hug.

"Neha!" Her mother pulled away abruptly and grabbed her face.

"Look at your head. What happened? "

"I—"

"You look dreadful, dear."

Neha made a face. "Really? And here I thought I looked my best before I walked out the door this morning. Mom, relax please before you go and get the nurses riled up... again. "

The woman wouldn't listen as she ran her hands through Neha's hair, unaware of all the hair she was pulling when it was caught up in a few stray knots.

"This is why I didn't think the train was a good idea." The mother shook her head. "This is exactly why."

"Mom, the train had nothing to do with it, alright? It's just been a stressful week at work and-"

"Well, we still have bills to pay."

"I can take care of that for you."

"No," her mom replied sternly.

She could feel the stress building in her chest and head as they began to ache. All she wanted to do was stay down and close her eyes, pretending that she was alone in the room.

Neha's mother opened her mouth to argue, but Neha turned on her side to ignore anymore conversation.

"Oh, alright." mother sighed. "Rest up, sweetheart."

The two left the room, leaving Neha alone, and she was glad, for at the moment, hot tears were streaming down her face and she didn't want her mother or sister to see her crying. It would only open up the floor for a million questions to be thrown at her. She was stressed; there was no denying that, but she was also tired, tired of the way she was being treated as if she were incapable of doing anything. She wasn't a child anymore, yet it seemed no one believed that because of her condition.

They didn't want her to be alone ever again, and they were trying to take everything that made her independent away from her. She was just supposed to sit around like some blob and have everyone do things for her while she did absolutely nothing.

6

The Late Night Therapy

It was near midnight when Jane finally found himself reaching his apartment, his eyes barely able to stay open as they had threatened to close numerous times on the way home. He unlocked the door to find Mourya sitting on the sofa watching television.

"Where have you been?" Mourya asked, sitting up and leaning forward as Jane walked in front of the television in the direction of an armchair. "It's near midnight."

"I'm aware," Jane said, sitting down. "I had to work late at the office."

"Again? What did you do this time? Breathe?"

"I was late again."

"The train?"

"Yes, the train was late and something else."

Mourya raised his eyebrows, "Something else? Well, don't just sit there, tell me what happened. "

"Neha."

"Oh, you talked to her, did you?" Mourya suddenly appeared giddy as he grabbed a pillow off the sofa and held it against his stomach and chest.

"No. I didn't. " Jane sighed.

"What about the note?"

"I left her a note."

"That's great!" Mourya lifted his arms triumphantly. His pillow fell to the ground without so much as a second glance. However, as he saw the look on Jane's face, the excitement faded from his expression as his arms dropped back down to his lap. "That's great, right?"

"No! I left her a note after she had a seizure on the train."

"You did what?"

"I-I-I was going to write her a simple little note, and when I looked up, she was on the floor on the train. "

"Having a seizure? but why-"

"Because she's epileptic, Mourya! But I was helping her. You know, she nearly drowned in her own spirit, from the looks of it. I stayed with her until we reached the station... then that wretch threatened me with my own job if I didn't come in. I had to leave her side... So I left her the note. "

"Did you leave your name and number at least?" Mourya asked, with a hopeful look in his eyes.

"I signed it Jane."

"That's it?! Jane! You're killing me, man!"

Jane started staring down at the floor, his leg shaking as he tapped his foot up and down in a nervous tick. His forehead was already beaded with sweat from describing the events of his day, reliving them all in his mind, much to his displeasure. He was already feeling short of breath but managed to keep talking to his friend.

"What else was I supposed to do, Mourya? Why would I leave my number? She probably would have been disgusted by the face of some man trying to pick her up while she was feeling ill. "

"Or maybe she would think about being able to meet the man who saved her life?"

"I wasn't thinking about that at the time. My main concern was that she was okay, once the medics assured me that, I wrote a note wishing her a speedy recovery and left to head to the office. "

Mourya sighed, falling back onto the couch. He had to hold back from yelling at his friend, knowing it would only turn Jane into a total mess.

"Why do you work for him?" Mourya finally asked.

"What?"

"Why do you work for that man, when all he does is make your life miserable?"

"I-I. He's my father, Mourya."

"No, he is not your father." He's a monster. He's been like that since we were kids and has done nothing but make your anxiety skyrocket anytime you're in his presence. For the love of God, Jane, he literally tortured you when you were eight years old because you were so upset about him yelling at you.He's not a father.

"He took care of me when my mom left."

"And that doesn't mean anything," Mourya said harshly. "He was supposed to take care of you. It was his duty as a father, not some chore. For God's sake, Jane, wake up. You could go out and get a good-paying job where they won't treat you like utter crap all the time."

"But if I quit, that means I give up and he wins."

"So, this is some sort of sick twisted little game that you two play? That's not healthy, dude, not at all. Do you want to wind back up in therapy again?"

"No" Jane replied with a shake of his head, "I don't."

"Then you need to get as far away from your dad as possible. You need to start thinking that you deserve to be happy, and soon things will start to get better. "

Jane nodded before looking up at Mourya with a half smile after a moment of silence passed by. "Since when did you become my therapist?"

"Look, I had a lot of wine earlier and have been watching a lot of television. There was some sort of marathon of Dr. Phil and I couldn't find the remote. "

"Perhaps you should go to bed, then?"

"Yeah, I'm going to go do that." Mourya pushed himself up and began shuffling down the hall.

"Night, Mourya."

"Night."

Jane pushed himself to stand and left his bedroom, removing his tie and then unbuttoning his dress shirt. His only relief was that he had the next day off. He showered, barely staying awake during the duration of shampooing his hair. Finally, he collapsed onto his bed and expected sleep to consume him easily, but he only found himself awake thinking of Neha.

He wondered if she was at her home or still in the hospital.

He wondered if he was going to get any sleep that evening.

More than likely, he would toss and turn until he dozed off and then his alarm would go off before his body relaxed enough to fall asleep. He had come later than usual, throwing his entire routine off, and he knew his mind was not going to let go of it so easily.

"Morning," Jane chuckled the next morning before taking a sip of his coffee. As his roommate stumbled out of his bedroom, the third cup of coffee that morning finally woke him up. He had been right about not getting any sort of sleep, but he couldn't use his lack of sleep as an excuse to show up late so he could sleep in. He would definitely lose his job as his father held no mercy, even if he was the man's son.

Mourya came into the kitchen rubbing his eyes and dragging his feet. There were dark bags under the man's brown eyes, making him appear half dead. He collapsed into one of the chairs and placed his forehead down on the table with a groan.

"I feel horrid."

"You look at it too." Jane pointed out.

"Thanks."

"You're welcome. That's what you get for finishing a whole bottle of wine by yourself. "

"I couldn't help it; it was so incredibly good. It comforted me, you know? They told me that I was so pretty and that I would be successful in life. That temptress."

"And where did that get you this morning?"

"With a headache from the deep depths of hell," Mourya said.

"Coffee?" Jane offered.

"No. I don't want to drink anything but water right now. "

Jane arose and grabbed his friend a cup of water. "Here."

"You ought to stop drinking anyway; it can't be good for your health," Jane told him.

"Yeah, yeah, my liver hasn't cried out for help yet."

Jane shook his head with a nervous laugh.

"And you said I looked like hell," Mourya countered, looking over at him. "Did you get any sleep last night?"

"Barely," Jane admitted. "I didn't fall asleep until around four."

"Then what the hell are you doing right now?"

"Well, I can't spend all day in bed."

"I can. Speaking of which, I think I hear my bed calling my name. " Mourya said. "Coming, Darling!"

7

Arjun

In the evening of the day she was discharged from the hospital, Neha sat outside on the small balcony attached to the apartment, allowing the cool night to relax her. Sasha was inside fumbling around in the fridge trying to figure out what to make for dinner and refused to let Neha help her. Rather than arguing, Neha just decided to remove herself from the situation and enjoy being out of the hospital bed that left her with horrible back pain.

With her sudoku book in her lap, Neha began trying to figure out the latest puzzle. She heard a knock at the front door of the apartment, bringing the woman to turn her head and peer through the glass door to see Sasha let Arjun in. She had no idea what her former friend was doing there; she certainly hadn't invited him over.

Neha sank into her chair to hide after releasing an irritated groan, cursing her sister for letting the man inside.

"She's out on the balcony." She heard Sasha say, giving her location away in a matter of seconds.

"Her and her big mouth," Neha growled as she heard footsteps approach and the door slip further open.

"Neha?" Arjun's voice called to her in a gentle tone.

"Yes?" she responded coldly. She was not about to let him walk back in and pretend everything was okay between them, because it was far from okay. She was furious. He had just dismissed her and told her to move her things because he was stressed out. Just the thought of it made her blood ill.

"Neha," he wandered over and sat across from her, "I heard you had a seizure on the train, and are you alright?"

"Why do you care?" she asked him simply. To many, it would appear that Neha was being extremely harsh to the man who was being so good to her, or acting to be good, but Neha knew she was in her right to treat him so. She wouldn't even give him the satisfaction of looking at him as she pretended to be fully concentrated on her puzzle.

"Why do I care? Neha, you could have been seriously hurt and look at your head. "

His large hand reached out and pushed a bit of her hair back, revealing the healing wound on her head. She pushed his hand away using her pen.

"Yeah, well, it's not a big deal. I'm fine. "

"Neha..." he began, "I've tried calling you on multiple occasions, I know you've received all my messages and voice mails."

"Your point?"

"My point is that I'm sorry for what I said. I realise I was wrong. I shouldn't have left you. "

"Right, well you didn't leave me, Arjun, remember? You insulted me. What has happened since I left? So now you come back for friendship?" She was questioned with venom dripping from her tongur.

"That's not true! Neha, I was scared when I said those things. "

"And what's changed now? Why, all of a sudden, are you so prepared to be with me again? If I remember correctly, Arjun, you told me I was too much for you to handle and that you needed to enjoy your life."

"I know what I said was horrible, Neha."

"You're damn right. It was horrible. I thought you were my friend, Arjun. "

"I made a mistake, Neha."

"Yes, you did. But I'm glad you did, Arjun, because it opened my eyes to what a farce our friendship really was. "

"A farce, that's what you think our friendship was?"

"Yes, Arjun, you deserve to live your life, without worrying about me, like you said."

"And what about you?"

"What about me?"

"Will you be okay?"

"Of course I will be. I've made it this far in my life, haven't I? "

Later on, Arjun left his tail tucked in between his legs, Sasha walked out with two plates of spaghetti, one for Neha and one for herself. She took a seat beside Neha, handing her a plate, and the two sat in silence for a few minutes.

"So, is it really over friendship between you?" Sasha finally asked her.

"Yes, I think it's for the best."

"He looked rather upset when he was leaving."

"And he will survive and move on." "I wish him all the best in finding the right woman for him." Neha told her.

"It doesn't matter; I'm not going to go looking for anything right now."For now, I'm going to eat this spaghetti and relax."

"What about this Jane fellow?" Sasha grabbed the note that was sitting inside of Neha's puzzle book.

"Well, as much as I want to find him, I don't think I'll be able to unless I go up to every person on the train and ask them if their name is Jane."

"Neha, you can't go back on the train, just let me drive you!" Sasha whined. "Please."

"At least for the first week you're back up and running, you should let me drive you."

"But if I'm stuck in the car with you, how am I supposed to meet Jane?"

"Leave that to me. I'm sure we'll be able to find him. "

"Without coming across as creepy, Sasha. For God's sake, please don't make the situation creepy. "

8

The Chance

Jane had hoped for any chance to see Neha on the train the following week, but by the fourth day, he realised he would probably never see her again. Perhaps the seizure scared the woman away from taking the train again, and Jane left a sort of devastation to take over him.He would never hear her laugh or watch her curse over her puzzle book, and that filled him with grief.

The second stop came on the fifth day, and she was nowhere in sight. Jane slumped in his seat, resting his head against the window of the train, and glancing out at the land as the train went past. It seemed fitting that he was wearing mostly all black as he sat in mourning over the death of his intelligence. He was internally scolding himself for not talking to Neha sooner or for not leaving any sort of contact information on the note. At least then he would have had a chance of ever talking to her again.

He arrived at the office five minutes early in the morning. Of course, he could see his boss staring at the clock as he entered. Mr. Krishnan said nothing before leaving for his office, making Jane sigh in relief as he walked over to his desk to set his things down.

"You look upset," Vishnu said. "She wasn't on the train again, I would presume?"

"No, she wasn't. I don't think she's going to get back on the train." Jane told him as he sat down.

"Well, you don't know that, Jane. She might just be recovering, you know? That's a strong possibility. She could still be in the hospital. Did you call to check? "

"I don't think they can give me that information, Vishnu. It's not like I'm family. I'm a complete and total stranger. I don't even know who I am. I can't just ask for information about her. That's going to make me come across as a complete nutter. "

"Or a man who's concerned for the well being of a person he helped save from a train." Vishnu smiled.

Jane rested his chin in the palm of his hand as his elbow was propped on his desk. "Perhaps it just wasn't meant to be."

After hours of typing in data and reviewing files, Jane's eyes were burning to close, but he could hear his father pacing around the building, scolding several employees for slacking off. All the while, he could hear Mourya's advice to quit and find something new, find a new job where he would be appreciated, and actually be happy for once. He turned over his shoulder and made eye contact with the man before facing his work.

He and his father shared the same eye color, but just looking at both sets of eyes, there was an obvious difference. His father's blue eyes were cold and distant, full of anger and resentment, especially whenever they looked over at Jane. Jane couldn't remember a time when they were bright and full of happiness, even when Jane's mother had been around.

The Krishnan household had never been a happy place, especially during Jane's childhood. He could remember the long nights where he would lie in bed wide awake, listening to his parents argue over anything and everything. Then, during the day, neither one of them could hardly stand to look at each other, let alone Jane.

Jane was the reason they remained together as long as they did, but Jane wished they hadn't, it certainly hadn't done any favours for him. It only created an even more hostile environment, and all the blame fell on him at the end, when his mother finally got separated.

It was during his childhood that Jane became so full of anxiety and his mind became repressed with troubling thoughts that weighed him down. The sounds of yelling, especially a male yelling, were enough to make Jane shake like a small dog in a submissive state. Jane's father had never physically hurt him, but the man didn't need to. The way he had ridiculed Jane as a child, the things that were said, had caused enough damage to Jane's mental health, enough so that Jane found himself working at his father's financial firm.

The apartment was eerily quiet that evening as Jane returned home. He knew Mourya wasn't working that late at the local restaurant, as it normally closed around nine. Normally, by that time, he was at home watching some sort of game on television. However, the game watching was normally accompanied by drunk yelling, cheering, or crying depending on the score.

He did hear the television on as he removed his jacket and hung it on a hook in the hall.

"Jane, is that you?" he heard Mourya call out.

"Who else would it be?" Jane replied.

"I'm coming." Jane loosened his tie as he headed towards the living room. But Mourya wasn't in his usual spot.

"Where are you?"

"I'm in the kitchen."

When Jane entered the kitchen, Mourya was sitting at the table with his laptop open.

"What's going on?" Jane asked him.

"Come here and check this out."

Walking around the table, Jane stood behind Mourya's chair and peered down at the screen. An article was pulled up on one of the news sites.

"Woman looking for a good Samaritan," he exclaimed before turning to face Mourya, who was beaming.

"No way," Jane said, shaking his head. "You're messing with me."

"Oh, no I'm not!" Mourya told him. "Look." Using the mousepad, he scrolled down the screen to pull up an image for Jane to look at. He leaned in to see a picture of the note he left with Neha.

"Neha Raj is seeking out the man named Jane who helped her out when she suffered a seizure on the train on her way to work. That's you, man!"

"She's looking for me?"

"Well, you're Jane, aren't you?"

Jane plopped into one of the chairs, just sitting in pure awe. He was sure his heart had stopped completely once or twice in the span of a minute. His breathing was picking up a faster pace, but he wasn't feeling terrible. In fact, he was actually quite excited until Mourya made a suggestion.

"You should contact the news station and tell them that you're Jane!" Mourya said.

All happiness, suddenly faded as Jane quickly shook his head.

"No."

"What?! Why not?"

"I... I don't know. Maybe I shouldn't tell her it was me."

Mourya rolled his eyes. "Jane, I love you, man, like you were my own brother, but sometimes I just want to punch you in the face. This is your chance, stupid, and if you let this one go, you'll probably never get another like this. Don't let it go."

9

The Interview

"Sasha, I don't think this was all necessary. I mean, I appreciate it and all, but it seems rather excessive, don't you think?" Neha frowned as she was curled up on the sofa with a blanket when she was supposed to be getting dressed and ready for the appointment that Sasha had booked. Unfortunately, when Neha told her sister to not go overboard and make the situation awkward and creepy, Sasha didn't listen and proceeded to do the complete opposite. In a few minutes, Sasha's friend, Jasira, who worked for the Newsday paper, would arrive to interview Neha about the incident on the train and the note.

"Do you want to find this Jane fellow or not?" Sasha asked her with an annoyed look, as she rested her hands on her hips.

"I do, but I don't want him to be frightened." Neha tried to reason with the woman, but it was like trying to reason with a stubborn child. "I might come across as a completely lunatic. There is a chance he left the letter because that's where he wanted to leave it, you know? Maybe he left it as just a polite gesture and nothing more. "

"Nonsense," Sasha waved her hand, completely dismissing the thought. "You are a gorgeous girl, and

I bet he would be thrilled to hear from you. It said 'Queen', not best wishes from Jane."

Neha rolled her eyes. "First off, looks have nothing to do with this, Sasha. He might have only signed his first name for a reason. I'm pretty sure he doesn't want to be contacted, and I really don't believe he wants this to go so far. I mean a news article? "

"What, I think it would be flattering."

Neha sighed at her sister's stubbornness."Yes, that's because you're actually insane. Alright, whatever, when is Jasira getting here? " She asked when there was a sudden knock at the door.

"NOW."

Jasira walked in with her leather bag strapped over her shoulder and a smile on her face before she took the seat that Sasha offered her.

"How are you, Neha? I haven't seen you since Sasha's birthday party. "

"Oh, I have been hanging in there," Neha replied. She really didn't want to think of the birthday party as everyone attending had given her looks of pity as she refused drink after drink of all the alcoholic beverages. Apparently, it was some adult crime not to drink, and when they learned of her medical condition, it was as if she had told them she only had until midnight and then she would be dead. One of Sasha's friends had become completely drowned-faced and ended up crying on Neha's shoulder for all of an hour because she felt so bad for Neha.

Neha had debated several times whether to push the woman into a closet and leave her for the remainder of the evening.

"I heard about the incident on the train," Jasira drew Neha out of her bitter thoughts, "Are you feeling better?"

"I feel fine, I felt fine back when I was at the hospital, but someone here is insistent that I rest all the time," Neha said, throwing a glance at her sister.

Jasira chuckled as she adjusted herself in the chair to make herself comfortable, her blonde curls bouncing as she moved. She looked so damn happy that Neha wondered if she could bottle some of it and keep it on her. She wished she could keep such a happy look on her face at all times.

"So, shall we get started?"

"Sure," she shrugged. What other choices did she have, honestly?

"Alright, tell me about the day on the train."

Neha began to tell the journalist about her seizure and how she awoke to find herself with a note in her hand.

"So you don't remember anything that happened during the seizure?" Jasira asked.

Neha raised her brow. "No, normally I don't. I tend to go unconscious during that time, so it's hard to recollect things. Sometimes I can hear the voices of the people around me, but not all the time. It really depends on the type of seizure I'm having."

Jasira's cheeks flushed a bright pink. "R-right. Can you actually feel when a seizure is about to come on? "

The interview was taking a turn as Jasira's curiosity got the better of her, while Neha's teeth were clenched in between her answers.

"I normally get a sense that they are coming because I can feel the aura."

"And what does that feel like?"

"Well, they never feel the same. Sometimes my toes tingle, other times I just get a bad feeling in my stomach... it's just something you can sense. But there are times when I get that feeling and then I don't have a seizure. My seizures aren't that bad usually. They just happened. "

She really didn't want to discuss it anymore, but she had to see the bright side of talking about her condition. The more people who knew about epilepsy, the less they would ask her.

"Alright, I feel like we might have drifted from the topic. That's my fault," Jasira said.

"It's okay," Neha reassured her, even though she wholeheartedly agreed.

"How about this note then?"

"I actually have it right here tucked away in my puzzle book," she said, reaching over to the coffee table. She took out the note and looked over it once more before handing it to Jasira.

Jasira took it carefully and reviewed it for a few seconds.

"Wow... this is really sweet," she said as she handed her the note back.For some reason, her tone sounded condescending to Neha, but perhaps it was just because she was in a foul mood.

"Do you mind if I take a picture of it before I leave?"

"Yeah, sure."

"So what do you want to happen from this interview?"

"I just want to find him so I can thank him. Face to-face,That's all. He did a really nice thing, and I just want him to know that it was really appreciated. " Neha told her.

"Well, hopefully, that will be the outcome. I'll write the article and send it to my editor. Then we'll get it out there, so we can find this Jane. "

"Thank you so much."

Once Jasira had gathered all the information she needed and wanted, she left, allowing Neha to retreat to her bedroom for the rest of the day to avoid Sasha. She ended up taking a long nap, and when she awoke, she decided to read a book to herself in the peaceful quiet. However, her sister just loved interrupting as she barged right in without so much of a knock.

"I have a question."

"The answer is if the door is there for you to knock on," Neha replied, looking up from her book.

"Yeah, yeah, shut up."

Sasha sat down on the edge of her sister's bed.

"What's your question, Sasha?" Neha asked her to set her book aside.

"Let's say you find this Jane. What are you going to do, just thank him and send him off on his merry way?"

"Uh... well yes. What am I supposed to do? "

"Maybe offer him some dinner, like a reward or something." Sasha shrugged.

"I guess I can do that if he wants to. I really don't want to make him feel awkward... but then again, this is even if we find him. Which I doubt we will. "

"You can be such a negative Nancy."

"I'm being a realist, thank you very much."

"Well, start thinking of places to take him out to eat, because you're going to find him," Sasha said before leaving the bedroom and turning the light off.

"I wasn't planning on going to sleep yet!" Neha yelled after her.

"Sleep tight!"

10

A Push in the Right Direction

"Are you going to work this morning?" Mourya asked casually as Jane walked into the kitchen, in the morning, fixing his tie. He was in a rush to get out the door, fumbling over the simplicity of just getting it around his neck. However, he was completely distracted by the obvious question that Mourya had called out to him.

"Mourya, I go to work nearly every morning. Why else would I be putting on a tie?"

"Sometimes I just think you like to dress fancy for no reason at all," Mourya grinned. "Some people like to dress up, you know? It makes them feel good. Anyways, I'm going to take the train with you today, then. "

"What?" Jane stopped, nearly choking himself with the tie as he looked over in the man's direction. "Why?"

"Because I want to head into the city for the day, there's absolutely nothing to do around here. If I just keep sitting around, I'm going to end up getting fat and I can't pick up the beauties with a pudge gut. "

"I'm not going to comment on whatever last part you just said, but you need to hurry up and get dressed, I'll be leaving in about fifteen minutes or so. If you're not ready, I'll leave without you. "

"What do you mean? I am dressed, "Mourya pointed to his attire with a pleased expression.

"Would you wear something else besides pyjama pants for once in your life?"

"Oh but they are so comfy," Mourya whined, leaving for his room, "You're not my real mom."

Jane shook his head as he heard Mourya slam his bedroom door playfully. Ignoring the childish play, he continued to fix the cut of his sleeve and stood before the mirror in the living room.

Jane did nothing about it since he read the article that announced Neha was indeed looking for him, Jane did nothing about it. Not because he didn't want to talk to Neha, but he was afraid if he actually met up with her, all he would do was to stand there and gape like an idiot. He found it so incredibly hard to talk to people that he had known for years. Approaching Neha would feel like a suicide mission.

Much to his luck, Neha hadn't been on the train, which also saddened him. His mind was absolutely torn. He wanted to talk to her, but he couldn't.

"Alright, let's go," Mourya said, returning about a minute later.

"You changed from pyjama pants to sweatpants." Jane sighed.

"I'm going for the casual look. You know, the I-don't-care-vibe. "

"Yeah, well, you're pulling it off tremendously."

"Excellent. Come on. "

Mr. Mourya sat beside Jane on the train, drumming his head against the seat before him, while Jane reviewed some files in his lap that had to be on Mr. Krishnan's desk that very morning.

"Do you really need to be doing all that work right now?" Mourya asked him.

"If I want to keep my job, yes," Jane answered, not bothering to even look up as they reached the second stop.

"You're a piece of work, you know that?"

"This would not be the first time, someone has said this to me." Jane chuckled. He jotted down something on a sticky note when his pen ran out of ink, "Of course."

"Oh no, he can't work anymore. What should he do?" Mourya said dramatically.

"Ha, lucky for me, I always have a bunch of spare pens with me."

"Of course you do."

Jane reached for his bag and pulled out a pen. As he pulled the cap off, he looked up and suddenly froze.

When Mourya looked over to make a quick remark, he saw Jane looking blankly ahead. His mouth slightly opened, his eyes widened.

"You alright, dude?"

When Jane didn't respond, Mourya lightly punched the man on the arm. Jane jerked his head and turned to Mourya.

"What's wrong?" Why do you have that face? "

"Because, Mourya... she's on the train," Jane said, barely a whisper.

Mourya looked around in an obvious manner. "Who is it?"

A few people glanced over at the two men before Jane hid his face behind his hands.

"It's the girl sitting in the first seat on the right side."

Mourya followed where Jane was looking and saw a petite girl sitting in one of the seats, talking on a cell phone.

"Are you sure?"

"What do you mean? Of course, I'm sure?"

"Well then, what the hell are you waiting for? Go over there and talk to her. "

"N-n-no. I couldn't do that. " Jane stammered.

"Why not Jane? She's been looking for you. This is your chance. You've been waiting for the prime opportunity to go and speak with her. Now grow some guts and go over there, right now! "

"I can't. I can't! " Jane shook his head frantically.

"Yes, you can. Say it with me, yes I can. "

Jane remained quiet.

Mourya sighed before pressing him back against the side of the train and pushing Jane out of his feet and hands. Jane nearly fell on another passenger seated across from them.

"Go" Mourya mouthed to him as Jane turned to him with a pleading look.

"Please don't make me do this."

"Go."

Jane could feel his entire body trembling as he inched towards where Neha was sitting. She had hung up her phone and was slouching in her seat after pulling over her puzzle book. He tried to calm his breathing by inhaling deeply and exhaling slowly. He looked over his shoulder to see Mourya motioning him to keep on going.

Finally, he stood beside Neha's seat, grabbing onto his jacket and running his fingers over the buttons in a soothing manner.

"Ex-e-excuse m-me?" he began.

Neha glanced up at him, and for the first time, he was able to observe her up close. Her hazel eyes met his, and for a moment, time seemed to stop around Jane.

He didn't move, he didn't speak, he didn't even blink.

"Are you alright?" her voice called out to him, bringing him back to earth.

"Err... Y-yes."

"Can I help you with something?" she asked with a small smile on her face.

"Um... I..." he scratched his forehead and rubbed the outside of his mouth. "Well, I..."

"Would you like to sit down?" she said with a quick pat on the seat beside her.

He could only nod his head.

Neha scooted over and moved her bags with her to allow the man to sit. Jane immediately sat as if his life depended on it and wrung his fingers in his lap.

"Are you sure you're okay?" she asked, turning her body to face him. He could hear the disbelief in her tone as he reassured her that he was just fine, but she didn't seem to want to argue with him.

He remained silent, allowing her to return her attention back to her book. Jane sat there wanting to throw himself out of the train because he was being so incredibly awkward around her. Even if he was coming across as a lunatic, he admired how kind she was being with him.

Out of concern, he could see the cut on her forehead was healing nicely from her fall. Her eyes were completely focused on the puzzle. He couldn't help but look down and realise that she had already made several mistakes. He didn't dare say anything though, the look of pure determination on her face deterred him. The perfume she was wearing was intoxicating, to say the least. It was light, a fragrance of some sort of flower that instantly began to calm Jane and his nerves. He assumed it was lavender as he often kept scented oils in the apartment when he needed to calm himself down and Mourya wasn't around to help.

He continued to sit in silence during the entire ride to the station, peeking over at her, but she didn't seem bothered by his presence.

When they came to their stop, Neha was the first to stand, collecting her things and throwing her book under her arm.

"You have a nice day," she wished him as she walked around him and left the train.

"You do the same!" He had finally found his voice, but once again, it was too late.

Mourya came up behind and clapped his hand on Jane's shoulder.

"What the hell was that?"

"I panicked."

"Yeah, no Sherlock."

11

A Cute Wuss

"Are you going to work this morning?" Mourya asked casually as Jane walked into the kitchen, in the morning, fixing his tie. He was in a rush to get out the door, fumbling over the simplicity of just getting it around his neck. However, he was completely distracted by the obvious question that Mourya had called out to him.

"Mourya, I go to work nearly every morning. Why else would I be putting on a tie?"

"Sometimes I just think you like to dress fancy for no reason at all," Mourya grinned. "Some people like to dress up, you know? It makes them feel good. Anyways, I'm going to take the train with you today, then. "

"What?" Jane stopped, nearly choking himself with the tie as he looked over in the man's direction. "Why?"

"Because I want to head into the city for the day, there's absolutely nothing to do around here. If I just keep sitting around, I'm going to end up getting fat and I can't pick up the beauties with a pudge gut. "

"I'm not going to comment on whatever last part you just said, but you need to hurry up and get dressed, I'll be leaving in about fifteen minutes or so. If you're not ready, I'll leave without you. "

"What do you mean? I am dressed, "Mourya pointed to his attire with a pleased expression.

"Would you wear something else besides pyjama pants for once in your life?"

"Oh but they are so comfy," Mourya whined, leaving for his room, "You're not my real mom."

Jane shook his head as he heard Mourya slam his bedroom door playfully. Ignoring the childish play, he continued to fix the cut of his sleeve and stood before the mirror in the living room.

Jane did nothing about it since he read the article that announced Neha was indeed looking for him, Jane did nothing about it. Not because he didn't want to talk to Neha, but he was afraid if he actually met up with her, all he would do was to stand there and gape like an idiot. He found it so incredibly hard to talk to people that he had known for years. Approaching Neha would feel like a suicide mission.

Much to his luck, Neha hadn't been on the train, which also saddened him. His mind was absolutely torn. He wanted to talk to her, but he couldn't.

"Alright, let's go," Mourya said, returning about a minute later.

"You changed from pyjama pants to sweatpants." Jane sighed.

"I'm going for the casual look. You know, the I-don't-care-vibe. "

"Yeah, well, you're pulling it off tremendously."

"Excellent. Come on. "

Mr. Mourya sat beside Jane on the train, drumming his head against the seat before him, while Jane reviewed some files in his lap that had to be on Mr. Krishnan's desk that very morning.

"Do you really need to be doing all that work right now?" Mourya asked him.

"If I want to keep my job, yes," Jane answered, not bothering to even look up as they reached the second stop.

"You're a piece of work, you know that?"

"This would not be the first time, someone has said this to me." Jane chuckled. He jotted down something on a sticky note when his pen ran out of ink, "Of course."

"Oh no, he can't work anymore. What should he do?" Mourya said dramatically.

"Ha, lucky for me, I always have a bunch of spare pens with me."

"Of course you do."

Jane reached for his bag and pulled out a pen. As he pulled the cap off, he looked up and suddenly froze.

When Mourya looked over to make a quick remark, he saw Jane looking blankly ahead. His mouth slightly opened, his eyes widened.

"You alright, dude?"

When Jane didn't respond, Mourya lightly punched the man on the arm. Jane jerked his head and turned to Mourya.

"What's wrong?" Why do you have that face? "

"Because, Mourya... she's on the train," Jane said, barely a whisper.

Mourya looked around in an obvious manner. "Who is it?"

A few people glanced over at the two men before Jane hid his face behind his hands.

"It's the girl sitting in the first seat on the right side."

Mourya followed where Jane was looking and saw a petite girl sitting in one of the seats, talking on a cell phone.

"Are you sure?"

"What do you mean? Of course, I'm sure?"

"Well then, what the hell are you waiting for? Go over there and talk to her. "

"N-n-no. I couldn't do that. " Jane stammered.

"Why not Jane? She's been looking for you. This is your chance. You've been waiting for the prime opportunity to go and speak with her. Now grow some guts and go over there, right now! "

"I can't. I can't! " Jane shook his head frantically.

"Yes, you can. Say it with me, yes I can. "

Jane remained quiet.

Mourya sighed before pressing him back against the side of the train and pushing Jane out of his feet and hands. Jane nearly fell on another passenger seated across from them.

"Go" Mourya mouthed to him as Jane turned to him with a pleading look.

"Please don't make me do this."

"Go."

Jane could feel his entire body trembling as he inched towards where Neha was sitting. She had hung up her phone and was slouching in her seat after pulling over her puzzle book. He tried to calm his breathing by inhaling deeply and exhaling slowly. He looked over his shoulder to see Mourya motioning him to keep on going.

Finally, he stood beside Neha's seat, grabbing onto his jacket and running his fingers over the buttons in a soothing manner.

"Ex-e-excuse m-me?" he began.

Neha glanced up at him, and for the first time, he was able to observe her up close. Her hazel eyes met his, and for a moment, time seemed to stop around Jane.

He didn't move, he didn't speak, he didn't even blink.

"Are you alright?" her voice called out to him, bringing him back to earth.

"Err... Y-yes."

"Can I help you with something?" she asked with a small smile on her face.

"Um... I..." he scratched his forehead and rubbed the outside of his mouth. "Well, I..."

"Would you like to sit down?" she said with a quick pat on the seat beside her.

He could only nod his head.

Neha scooted over and moved her bags with her to allow the man to sit. Jane immediately sat as if his life depended on it and wrung his fingers in his lap.

"Are you sure you're okay?" she asked, turning her body to face him. He could hear the disbelief in her tone as he reassured her that he was just fine, but she didn't seem to want to argue with him.

He remained silent, allowing her to return her attention back to her book. Jane sat there wanting to throw himself out of the train because he was being so incredibly awkward around her. Even if he was coming across as a lunatic, he admired how kind she was being with him.

Out of concern, he could see the cut on her forehead was healing nicely from her fall. Her eyes were completely focused on the puzzle. He couldn't help but look down and realise that she had already made several mistakes. He didn't dare say anything though, the look of pure determination on her face deterred him. The perfume she was wearing was intoxicating, to say the least. It was light, a fragrance of some sort of flower that instantly began to calm Jane and his nerves. He assumed it was lavender as he often kept scented oils in the apartment when he needed to calm himself down and Mourya wasn't around to help.

He continued to sit in silence during the entire ride to the station, peeking over at her, but she didn't seem bothered by his presence.

When they came to their stop, Neha was the first to stand, collecting her things and throwing her book under her arm.

"You have a nice day," she wished him as she walked around him and left the train.

"You do the same!" He had finally found his voice, but once again, it was too late.

Mourya came up behind and clapped his hand on Jane's shoulder.

"What the hell was that?"

"I panicked."

"Yeah, no Sherlock."

12

Bright Pink Wig

"Why are you wearing that wig on your head?" Jane asked as he arrived home from work to see Mourya sitting at the kitchen table with a bright pink wig on. One year, Mourya decided to dress up as Nymphadora Tonks from Harry Potter for Halloween, although no one at the party knew who he was. They just assumed that he had gone as a crossdresser of some sort, leaving Mourya oddly bitter for the entire night.

"Because I'm going to help you," Mourya answered, tucking a lock of his pink hair behind his ear.

"Have you been drinking again?" Jane said as he approached him cautiously.

"I might have had a few sips here and there, but that's not the point. The point is, you missed a huge opportunity to talk to Neha today. "

Jane frowned.

"She was right there, you actually sat next to her and then you froze. You can't do that, Jane. "

"It's not like I wanted to, Mourya. I didn't ask to be this pathetic in life. "

"Well, I know that that's why I put on this wig."

"To scare me into talking to her?"

"No, I want you to pretend I'm Neha and have a conversation with me. Right here, right now. " Mourya proceeded to grab oranges from the small fruit basket at the centre of the table and stuff them down his shirt to give him the appearance of a girl.

VERY ODD.

"I am not doing that." Jane laughed, removing his jacket and throwing it over the back of the sofa. He loosened his tie while Mourya turned to him with an offended look.

"And why not? I think I cleaned up quite nicely. "

"Well, for one, Neha doesn't have pink hair, so it's going to be hard to visualise you as her with that distracting hair. And two, I know you're not Neha, you are Mourya. I've known you since we were kids. It's obviously going to be a lot easier to talk to you than it is with her. Even if you are half drunk and wearing a wig. "

"Sit," Mourya demanded, pulling out the chair beside him.

Jane rolled his eyes up at the ceiling before walking over and plopping down next to Mourya.

"No, no Get up! You have to ask to sit near me. "

"But you just said... oh never mind!" After biting the inside of his cheek, the man stood up and stood beside the chair.

"Now, I want you to pretend we're on the train." Mourya instructed him, fumbling with one of his false figures.

"Alright, we're on the train."

Jane was too distracted by Mourya fluttering his eyelashes.

"Please stop being so distracting," Jane said. "Neha doesn't look at me like that and she certainly doesn't have any figures like that... thank God."

Well, get on with it. I'm not getting any younger here. "

Jane sighed."May I sit next to you?"

"No," Mourya replied.

"No? What do you mean no? "

He patted the chair beside him. "I'm just messing with you. Please have a seat," he said.

"I can't believe we are doing this."

Mourya grinned and then stared at Jane.

"Why are you looking at me like that?" Jane inquired.

"I'm waiting for you to make small talk with me."

"About what?"

"Well, you could start off by asking me about work or complimenting me on my hair."

"I highly doubt that on her way to work, Neha is going to want to talk about work."

"Then compliment me on my hair!" Mourya yelled.

Jane leaned away. "Er.. your hair looks lovely."

"Oh why, thank you. I was going for the look of bubblegum. "

"And you pulled it off quite nicely."

"See? Now was that so hard? " Mourya asked him.

"Mourya, you and Neha are nothing alike. This isn't good practice. In my mind, I know it's you in a flamboyant wig. You're loud and crazy, while Neha is much more focused on her puzzles, I doubt she wants to just hear some compliments on her hair. I'm sure she gets enough of that from other people. "

Mourya folded his arms. "You tell me all this and yet you can't start a conversation with her about scenery or her puzzles?"

"I don't want to bother her."

"You can't bother her, Jane, she's looking for you! Once you tell her that it's you, I'm sure she's going to be thrilled. I am thrilled that the man that saved her, is a nice, respectable gentleman that will go well with her quiet and reserved demeanor. " Mourya said, pulling off the wig.

"But every time I have ever tried to speak with her, I just can't think of anything to say."

"You said she works on her puzzles every morning, so talk about the puzzles. Better yet, get a damn puzzle book yourself and work on it next to her. Don't even bother asking her to sit. When you sit beside her, whip out your puzzle book and let everything go from there. Instead of going after her, let her come to you. "

"But you just said..."

"Just listen to me, Jane. Tomorrow morning, we're both going on that train and you are going to talk to her, because if you don't, I will personally go to her and introduce you."

"No... don't do that."

"I will if you don't nut up. You know the rules, it's nut up or shut up and I'm not allowing you to stay quiet any longer. "

"Don't you have to work tomorrow?" Jane pointed out.

"I guess I'm calling in sick."

Jane glared at Mourya, who sat across from him on the train. Jane planned on getting up exactly early to catch an earlier train to avoid the whole scenario altogether, but Mourya knew him all too well. He was up at the crack of dawn waiting for Jane in the living room.

So there they were sitting opposite of each other, waiting to arrive at the second stop. With Mourya wearing a ridiculously bright pink wig because, as he explained it, he was going "incognito." But Jane had reminded him countless times that Neha had no idea who he was, so there was no point in him disguising himself. He was just beginning to think that Mourya was looking for any sort of excuse to wear it.

Jane hoped in the beginning that Neha wouldn't board the train that morning. But then he knew all too well that he would be worried if she didn't. He would spend the entire day wondering if she was alright.

The train came to a halt, and Jane could feel his hands starting to tremble in his lap. Talking on a phone at work was much different than talking to a person face-to-face, especially one that Jane found incredibly attractive. He had known his co-workers for a long period of time, so it was easy to talk to them as well. However, Neha was a whole other playing field.

Mourya gave him a look, and Jane glanced over to see Neha board the train. She wasn't on her cellphone, in fact, her eyes were up and alert as they scanned the train. He waited for her to walk over to her usual seat, but to his surprise, she sat beside him.

Jane could see Mourya grinning. Meanwhile, he felt like he was going to pass out as he held his breath.

"Good morning," Neha spoke.

He turned his head and saw her smile at him.

Oh, the smile that made his knees weak and his heart beat harder than anything.

"M-m-morning," he returned the greeting.

Perhaps sensing his nerves, she said nothing more before folding her hands in her lap and looking out the window.

Mourya was signalling to him to say something, but Jane continued to shake his head no.

His best friend threatened him by standing up, but Jane quickly turned to Neha.

"Your hair looks lovely!" he blurted out.

13

Very Good at Numbers, not very good at talking

The morning didn't start off on a good note for Neha either. Like many other girls, she struggled to find something to wear that morning that would flatter her figure. But no matter what she threw on from her closet, she seemed to be drowning in all her clothing. Frustrated with the fact that she had fit into the same clothing months prior, she sat down on the floor in her bedroom, almost in tears.

Sasha walked in to see if Neha wanted any breakfast to find her sister on the floor with her hands over her face while she was shaking her head.

"Neha, what's wrong? Are you feeling okay? "

Neha shook her head as her voice cracked as she spoke.

"Nothing fits. All my clothes are too big. They used to fit a few weeks ago, but now everything is just too big. "

Sasha walked over and sat down beside her. "Well, if it makes you feel any better, most women would love to have that happen to them."

"No. That doesn't make me feel any better! " Neha told her. "I didn't want to lose weight in the first place, and all this diet is doing is to make me lose it."

"But the doctor said it would help."

"I don't care what the doctor said. Look at me, Sasha. I'm a bloody skeleton right now. The only thing that seems to fit right now is my skin, and I'm pretty sure that's going to end up being too big if I keep losing weight. "

Neha lifted up her shirt, exposing her ribs that were sticking out.

"Does that look healthy to you? Look at my arms. Look at me. I feel absolutely disgusted right now. "

Sasha pulled her sister into a tight hug. "You may feel it, but you don't look disgusted at all, Neha." You look beautiful. If losing the weight bothers you this much, then you should call the doctor's office and setup an appointment. Perhaps this diet isn't one for you, or maybe they can tweak it so you're not losing all this weight. There has to be something they can do. "

Neha nodded her head, wiping at her eyes. "Yeah, I should do that."

"In the meantime, I'm sure some of this clothing is bound to fit you. I'll get some safety pins and perhaps we can fix something up. Alright? "

"Yeah, alright."

When Sasha left the room, Neha immediately felt anger with herself. Once again, she came across as helpless to her sister. It looked like she couldn't even pick out an outfit that morning without some help. She pushed herself up and picked up the closest well-fitting dress she owned and put it on before Sasha returned. She waited patiently as Sasha took in some of the fabric to give it a tighter fit. However, as she stared at herself in the mirror, she frowned as she noticed her ribs sticking out still.

"Can you make it a little looser?" she asked, looking down at her feet. Sasha nodded her head and adjusted the dress a little bit more.

"There, that should do it." It looks great. I should have gone into fashion designing."

Neha chuckled, looking in the mirror once more. "Thank you, Sasha."

"Anytime. Now hurry up before you're late for the train. Unless you want me to take you-"

"Nope!"

Neha quickly fixed her hair into the fastest ponytail and headed out the door for the station.

She was surprised as she waited at the stop that Mr. Daniel hadn't bothered calling her with his daily coffee order, but Neha wasn't complaining either. It probably just meant he called Hannah or one of the other girls to do it. It was certainly a break that was well needed from the insufferable man.

Finally, the train arrived, and Neha stepped on. Her eyes immediately focused on the awkward man who sat beside her the day prior. She smiled to herself before taking the seat beside him.

"Good morning." she said in a soft voice in hopes of not startling the poor man.

He looked over at her. His blue eyes seemed so fazzled as they darted back and forth. She could see how hard he swallowed before he spoke.

"M-m-morning."

His voice shook in a way that made Neha's heart break just hearing it. She wondered why he came across as so scared. His hands shook as much as his voice did. She pressed her lips together and decided to look out the window, trying to figure out what to say to him. It was like his nervousness was contagious as she began to fidget beside him, regretting her bold choice of sitting next to him.

Suddenly, he said something, causing her to jump as she was startled out of her thoughts.

She turned her head to him.

"What did you say?" she asked.

His face was losing all colour and he looked very close to nausea.

"I-I said y-your hair... it looks lovely," he whispered.

"O-oh!" The man had caught her completely off guard with the compliment. "Why, thank you."

He nodded his head before looking away.

There was another man seated across from them, who seemed to be watching the scene unfold as he shook his head before smacking his forehead.

Neha ignored him and returned her attention to the awkward stranger.

"My name is Neha," she introduced herself, hoping it would make things less weird between them.

The man didn't say anything; he just began to tap his foot up and down.

Not wanting to overwhelm him, Neha sat quietly, pulling out her puzzle book. She would watch him out of the corner of her eye as he would peer over slightly and watch her work the puzzle. Every time she wrote down one of the numbers, he would make a facial expression. His eyebrows would knit together, he would scrunch up his face, or he would give a slight nod as if he was trying to help her without saying a word.

At one point, she wrote down the number and his face only made her laugh. He obviously did not like her choice. She closed the book and turned so that her whole body faced him.

"I take it you're very good at sudoku," she said.

He nodded.

"And by your facial expression, it's safe to assume that I'm not very good at Sudoku."

He shook his head, making her laugh again.

"Would you like to help me then?"

Another nod

"Alright," she smiled, opening up the book again. Following his facial expressions, Neha worked on the puzzle and, in no time, completed one of the pages.

"Wow, you really are good with these."

The train came to its final stop. Neha quickly placed the puzzle book away and arose as people prepared to leave the train. She placed her bag strap on her shoulder and faced the man, but he was quickly moving for the exit.

"Wait!" She hurried after him and touched his shoulder lightly. He glanced over his shoulder, his eyes wide.

"I never got your name," she said.

He cleared his throat and pulled at the collar of his button-up.

"I.I., I'm Jane."

14

Jane's Breaking Point

Neha's eyebrows knitted together in confusion after Jane confused his name for her. All the while her eyes trailed over him, he felt as though they were looking directly into his soul. The way she looked at him caused him immediate discomfort as he anxiously began to seek an escape route. He knew she wasn't expecting him to be the man that saved her. Neha had expected a knight in shining armor, a prince charming, but Jane was no prince, and he wasn't a knight either. He was more of the kind that members of the king's court laughed at.

No, he was a man that became intimidated far too easily in the presence of people. Rather than brushing off looks and whispers, Jane became trapped in his mind. Struck with no words to explain himself, When the anxiety took over, everything felt like it was over to Jane. He thought back to the technique his therapist had once informed him of; grounding was what she had called it.

FIVE

He could see five things. He could see the necklace Neha was wearing, the trains moving in the background, a woman pulling her child along, a man eating his breakfast on the go, and lastly, his shoes.

FOUR

Four things he could hear, A child crying, the sound of the tacks, a laugh in the distance, and Neha repeating his name.

THREE

Three things he could touch. He touched the button of his jacket, ran his finger over the scar of his arm, and then he pulled at a lock of his own hair.

TWO

Two things he could smell. He could smell Neha's perfume and his own.

ONE

Take one deep breath. Jane inhaled slowly and exhaled.

He returned his attention to Neha to see her rummaging through her bag for something. She was distracted, and he saw his opportunity to flee. Backing away slowly, he disappeared among the crowd of people, hiding away from further embarrassment.

He hid behind a cold wall after finding the perfect spot to hide and buried his face in his hands. He could hear footsteps approaching him and prayed it wasn't Neha.

"Dude, what are you doing?" Mourya's voice greeted his ears. Jane felt some sort of relief as he looked up to his friend, but Mourya didn't look very pleased with him. "You left her back there."

"I know! I know! B-b-but but... "

Mourya knelt down in front of him. "It's alright Jane, just breathe, okay? It's not a big deal. You're fine, we're in the train station, and I'm right here. "

Jane nodded his head, already feeling the perspiration that was starting up from his body temperature rising. A few people passing by gave the men weird looks until Mourya shooed them off.

"You said to her it was you, huh?" Mourya asked.

"Yeah," Jane said. "I did. But you should have seen the way she looked at me. "

"It couldn't have been that bad."

"She looked disappointed. Like she didn't want it to be me. "

"I don't think that's true at all. Jane. I think you just panicked and you let your own insecurities get the best of you. Maybe that was just too much for one day."

"She probably thinks I'm pathetic."

"No-"

"Look at me, Mourya! I'm sitting on the floor of a train station with my head tucked in between my legs, because the girl that I've been dying to talk to finally said something to me and I couldn't handle it. I ran off and she probably thinks I'm insane. "

"I think you handled yourself rather well on the train." She was smiling and laughing the entire time.

"Yes, at me."

"No, not at you. Well, sort of at you, not in a bad way. She wouldn't have asked you for your name if she didn't want to continue talking to you. "

"Well, it doesn't matter because she's never going to want to talk to me again. I just ran off on her. "

"If she's as good as you say she is, I don't think she's going to hold it against you."

Jane remained silent, and they sat there for a little while longer. Suddenly, panic filled Jane's chest.

"What time is it?"

" A quarter after nine, why-?"

"Shut!" Jane jumped up. "I'm fckng late, Mourya!"

"Jane, wait! Slow-" It was no use, though, as Jane was long gone. He sighed with a shake of his head. "Hopefully, Mr. Krishnan is feeling some sort of mercy today, but I doubt it."

Jane ran through the doors but came to a screeching halt as his father stood before him with his hands crossed, glaring at his watch.

"Sir-I-"

"Save it, Jane," Mr. Krishnan said. "I told you what the consequences would be if you were late again, and here we are."

Jane looked at the floor, unable to meet his father's eyes.

"You're fired."

"N-no, you can't do that! You don't understand. "

"I don't care," Mr. Krishnan began.

"I'm your son!" Jane yelled at him, causing everything to fall silent. "I'm your goddamn son. How could you do this to me?"

A few of the workers in the building came around the corner to observe the scene. Mr. Krishnan didn't look at all phased by his son losing his temper, and while Jane would have normally become nervous and start apologizing, he had finally snapped.

"Son or not, you didn't follow the rules."

"Don't talk to me like that. I'm some sort of child... following the rules... I had an anxiety attack while at the train station this morning! But you don't care... not one bit. "

"Your mental health is your responsibility and"

"You're the one who does this to me!" Jane threw an accusing finger in the man's face. "You made me like this! I can't even have a normal conversation with a stranger because of you. "

"Do not blame me for-"

"I will certainly blame you! I blame you for not treating me like a human being my entire life! I have grown up thinking I'm this inferior thing to the world. All because you couldn't show me an ounce of respect. After all, I've tried to make you show me some sort of respect. You think I wanted to work for you? Of course not! But I did... I did so in the hopes that one day you could look me in the eye and see me as your equal. As your son. "

The whole office was silent as the two men stared down each other. Jane tried to keep eye contact with his father, but he faltered, looking down.

"But it's not worth it," Jane said softly. "It's just not worth it anymore. Now I see why my mother left. "

"How dare you?"

Jane lifted his hand, causing his father to stop. "Goodbye." was all that he said before walking out of the office building.

He stood outside on the side walk and looked up at the sky, letting out a sigh of relief until he realised that he was suddenly unemployed.

15

The Invitation

Neha couldn't believe her eyes when the man introduced himself as Jane. She realised she probably looked like a gaping fish, but she didn't understand how crazy it was to figure out he was Jane all along. She went to dig into her bag to pull out the note to confirm that he was Jane. Her hands trembled as she searched for it, cursing herself under her breath for not keeping her bag cleaner.

"Ah ha!" She pulled it out, but as she turned to hand it to him, Jane was gone.

"Jane?"

She looked all around, standing on her tiptoes, but the man was nowhere in sight. She frowned, completely puzzled by the man's behaviour. He had introduced himself, only to run off. The man was so confusing to Neha. It was like he wanted to talk to her but then he didn't. She knew she had to head to work, but she wanted to make sure he was alright as well.

Unsure of what else to do and glancing down at her watch, Neha knew she had to go or she was going to have to face Mr. Daniel. She slipped the note back into her bag and went to leave the station.

"Neha?" she heard her name called as she reached the steps. She turned around and saw a familiar man running towards her. She recognised him from the train as the one who continued to facepalm in her direction when she was speaking to Jane.

"Neha, right?"

She eyed him suspiciously, hoping that he wasn't going to make any snide or rude remarks about Jane. So many times, when a man approached her, they often liked to degrade another person as if it made them look better. "Yes?"

"I'm Mourya. I..." the man said, completely winded. He placed his hands on his knees as he bent over to catch his breath. "One sec.. I'm a bit out of shape."

Neha waited patiently as the man gathered himself. Finally, he stood straight, exhaling loudly.

"Hi. I'm Mourya. " He introduced himself again, holding his hand out to her. She took it and shook it gently, still keeping an arm's length between them until he explained what he wanted.

"Nice to meet you, Mourya," she replied politely. "I hope this doesn't come across as rude, but what do you want?"

"I'm Jane's friend," he informed her.

"You are?" Her eyes lit up."Do you know where he left for? I was just talking to him and then he was gone. "

"He was late for work. His boss is a total prick if he's late."

"Oh! Well, I totally understand that. I just wanted to give him the proper thank you about-"

"The note?"

She furrowed her brow. "How do—"

"Jane knows you've been looking for him."

"He does?"

"Yes... it's just... you need to understand that Jane is very shy."

"Gee, I hadn't noticed." She smiled.

"It goes beyond making conversation; he has really bad anxiety. So he wasn't sure how to approach you. "

"Well, I never wanted him to feel so anxious. Like I said, I only wanted to thank him for all that he did. Everyone told me how great he was. Once I woke up, I really just wanted to thank him face-to-face because most people probably wouldn't have known what to do. "

Mourya smiled in return. "He really is a great guy, and I think he wants to talk to you a bit more, but perhaps somewhere a bit more private."

"Uh, okay," Neha nodded. "I can do that. If it'll help him not get so worked up. "

"Great, look. I'll give you the address and you can stop by. I think he'll be much more comfortable and relaxed in the apartment. "

"Go to the apartment?" She was hesitant about showing up at a man's house, especially since she didn't really know him that well. But Jane seemed so genuinely nice that she really shouldn't find herself refusing. "Alright, yeah, that's no problem."

"Do you have a pen and paper?"

"Er, yes!" she said, digging into her bag and pulling the supplies out.

Mourya quickly jotted it down for her.

You are welcome to come whenever you want, but he should be home when you get off work.Hopefully, he won't be working late."

"Hopefully, thanks you so much! I honestly can't thank you enough. "

"Don't mention it. I'm sure Jane will be happy to see you. "

"I hope so." She glanced down at her watch again. "I'm sorry. I don't mean to be rude, but I have to head to work myself. "

"Oh! Right, go on! See you later! "

"Bye!" she waved, running up the stairs.

Neha arrived at the office and snuck over to the desk with a smile on her face as she set her things down.

"Neha, where have you been?" Hannah said as she walked over.

"Sorry, I know I'm late," Neha began, "but you wouldn't believe what happened this morning."

"Well, out with it!"

"I found Jane!"

"What?"

"I know it's crazy. But he actually sat next to me on the train without me knowing, and... when I asked him what his name was, he introduced himself as Jane. and there's more! "

"What else could there be?"

"He's the shy gentleman from the other day."

"Wait a second, the Wuss is Jane?"

"For the last time, Hannah, he's not a Wuss. He's just shy and he has a few problems when it comes to dealing with his anxiety. That's understandable. "

"Alright, whatever you say. So, what else happened? Did you guys exchange numbers? "

"No, he ran off before I could really talk to him."

"Oh for the love of"

"However," Neha continues, "his roommate met me at the station and gave me the address to their apartment so I could go there and thank him."

"Um... I don't think that's a good idea." Hannah frowned.

"What? Why not? "

"Well, it could be a set up to hurt you, Neha." "You're a pretty girl going to an apartment all alone."

"Why must you force the negatives?"

Neha sighed.

"I'm just being realistic, sweetheart. I don't want to see you get hurt. "

"Then I won't go by myself. I'll have Sasha take me or something. Even though I'm sure I would be perfectly fine because I don't think Jane and Mourya are complete lunatics. "

"That makes me feel better. Before I forget, if Mr. Daniel asks you, you've been in the washroom, you ate something this morning that did not agree with you."

"Thanks, Hannah."

"Anytime."

16

Internal struggle of mind

Jane wasn't sure what he had exactly done when he arrived back at his apartment, as he was in a bit of shell shock. He was aware that he had finally stood up for himself against his father. But he hadn't come to terms that he had been fired. There was no way he was going back to beg for his job either. He meant what he said. He just didn't want to see his father again. It was goodbye for good. At least, that's what he hoped it meant.

For some reason, it didn't hurt him to think of not having his father in life. In fact, the thought made him happy, as if the weight of the world had finally been lifted from his shoulders, no longer holding him down or back. No longer would he be ridiculed for absolutely nothing or for things that were clearly out of his control. He was free, and now he only wished he had done it sooner.

Jane felt completely pathetic upon entering the apartment. He didn't feel like a human at all, let alone a man. He felt like a coward. Setting his things down to the side, Jane proceeded to walk over to the couch and plop down, not having to worry about taking Mourya's spot as the man still appeared to be out for the day.

There was no way he was going to be able to face Neha at that point. He couldn't form coherent sentences around her, not to mention he could hardly breathe. Neha deserves better than that. She deserved a strong person that she could lean on and depend on when she needed to.

A while later, Jane was still in the same spot when Mourya came into the apartment. The man stopped in the doorway, confused to see Jane home so early.

"What are you doing?" Mourya asked him.

"I got fired today." Jane replied flatly, staring at the television that wasn't even on at that moment.

"Why?"

"Because I was late and because Mr. Krishnan is a total prick."

Mourya raised his brows at the hostility in Jane's voice.

"Ohhh-"

"Then I snapped." Jane said.

"You what?"

"I snapped. I lost my temper. How else do you want me to phrase it?"

Mourya grinned."You let him have it, didn't you?"

While he wasn't expecting it, Jane wouldn't deny that a hug felt good in that moment as Mourya pulled him into one and bounced up and down in place, just full of pure excitement.

"What did he say after you told him all that?" Mourya questioned. "You just walked out?"

"I did."

"Whoo! That's awesome, man! You don't know how happy that makes me. You just should have told him to go to hell and it would have been absolutely perfect. Well, you did the right thing, Jane. Do you feel better? "

"Yes and no."

"What's the catch?"

"I feel terrible for leaving Neha standing there like that."

"Oh Jane, don't worry about that! I took care of it. "

Jane froze. "Mourya, what did you do?"

"I may have given her our address so she could come talk to you... tonight."

"You did what?" Jane jumped up. "Mourya!"

Mourya witnessed Jane run to the kitchen as if he was going to get away that easily. The man was gripping the counter where he walked in, trying to keep himself standing as panic was washing over him in waves comparable to an incoming tide.

"Listen, it's going to be okay, Jane. You're going to be in the comfort of your own home. It should make it easier on you. "

"No it won't, Mourya. Don't you get it? I just can't. "

"You can. You told her your name. You told her she had lovely hair. You're welcome, by the way. You can talk to Jane. You have to keep saying you can because you already have. "

"Why would she even agree to come here and speak with me? Does she not realise that the man that helped her on the train is nothing more than a coward? "

Mourya sighed and shook his head, bringing Jane over to sit on one of the chairs around the kitchen table. Jane nearly fell back into the chair as he completely lost feeling in the lower part of his legs. "You really need to stop thinking like that, Jane. It isn't healthy for your mental health. "

"But it's true."

"No, it isn't," Mourya said. "It's not true at all. It's just all this nonsense that you have trapped up there in that weird little head of yours. "

"You think she'll come?" Jane asked him, looking up before he ended up with a bald patch.

"I know she'll come," Mourya reassured him. "Now go to your room and calm down. You need to relax before you have a heart attack. Or do I have one for that matter? God, you know how to get people worked up. I was doing just fine and how you got me questioning myself. "

"Like what?"

"Like, do I look chubby in these pants?"

Jane tried to relax in his bedroom by laying on his bed, but he was still nervous about Neha coming. His mind was full of thoughts pertaining to what she was going to think about him.

Did she think that he was a full-grown man not living on his own?

What would she think of the apartment? Was it too dull? Was it neat enough? Not messy enough?

Jane's mind was his greatest weakness because he was not in control of his own thoughts. He couldn't tell himself what to think, as if his brain was a separate entity that he had no control over. Jane was constantly at odds with himself and was always on the losing end.

Dozing off from pure exhaustion of stress, Jane awoke when he heard a knock at the door.

Mourya poked his head. "Oh good, you're awake. She's here. "

"She is?"

"Yes, do you want me to answer the door, or do you want to?"

Jane thought for a second before standing up.

"I'll answer it."

17

The Question

"Are you sure you want to do this, Neha?" Sasha asked as she pulled up the car outside the address given. She turned the car off and faced her younger sister, who was glancing out of the passenger side window, looking up at the apartment building.

"Will you stop me?" "Yes, I'm sure." Neha said, turning back to her. "If I wasn't, we wouldn't be here right now. I really want to do this, okay? "

"You have your cellphone on you, correct?"

"Yes."

"Alright, well if anything happens, just call me and I'll be right there!"

"Yes, mom! Can I go now? " Neha huffed before opening the door and stepping out. Throughout the entire trip, it had been the same question over and over.

"I'll be right out here!" Sasha yelled after her through the open window.

Neha froze for a moment. She shook her head in embarrassment and then headed up the stairs quickly before Sasha could yell anything else. She heard feet shuffling behind the door and then whispering. She leaned her head in a little to see if she could hear what they were saying, but it was all too muffled for her to actually understand anything.

"Hello?" she called out.

The door knob jiggled for a moment before the door finally opened and Jane stood there, looking down at the ground.

"H-h-hi Neha," he said in a small voice, as if he were a child about to be scolded by a parent.

"Hello, Jane. May I come in?" she asked.

"Of course." He quickly moved aside to let her in. She saw Mourya, who smiled in his direction with a nod of his head before leaving for his room.

She wandered inside and looked around the apartment. It was incredibly neat and tidy. Nothing seemed out of place. She turned around and faced Jane, who was threading his fingers on the bottom of his shirt.

"Umm.... I wanted to come here and thank you. " She began pausing for a moment to allow him to respond. Eventually, he looked up at her when he realised that she was no longer speaking, but he didn't say anything.

"When I woke up, I had your note in my hand. A woman told me you helped me, and when I got to the hospital, I read your note fully. "

"I wanted to stay." Jane responded quitely. "But I couldn't."

"I completely understand," she told him.

"You do?"

She nodded. "My boss is a real stickler for being on time as well. I wouldn't expect people to stay. Normally, I recover very quickly. "

"But you hit your head..."

"Yeah, sometimes that happens," Neha replied, scratching her head awkwardly. "Most of the time, I can feel one coming and I'll just sit down and prepare myself for it, but I just didn't have a warning this time. I hope I didn't scare you too much. "

Once again, Jane didn't say anything, and she figured that she probably did scare him or at least make him feel uncomfortable about the whole situation. Suddenly, her idea appeared rather stupid, and she was left standing there, shuffling her feet nervously like an idiot.

"I... I am sorry." Jane said to her.

"Why? You've done nothing wrong. "

"I'm not very good at starting conversations, if you haven't noticed."

Neha smiled. "That's okay. I won't take up any more of your time. I just really wanted to thank you for being so kind. "

She walked towards the door, unsure of what was left to say. She didn't want him to feel any more uncomfortable in his own home.

"You're welcome," Jane said.

She opened the door. "Well, I guess I'll see you around on the train. You're more than welcome to join me for sudoku. "

He nodded.

"Have a nice night," she muttered before walking out.

"You do the same," Jane called after her as Neha closed the door.

Mourya poked his head around the corner. "Jane, you've got to be kidding me?"

"What?" He spun around to face his friend who was looking at him in disapproval.

"Go out there and ask to get some lunch or something!" Mourya said.

"What?NO!I-"

"Jane, you march out there right now or so help me, I will kick you."

"What do I even say?"

"Neha, would you like to have lunch with me? Boom, simple, done. That's all you have to say. "

"What if she says no?"

"What if she says yes?"

Jane couldn't argue with it as Mourya ran over and pushed him out the door. "I'm not letting you in until I hear you ask her."

Jane went to protest, but Mourya closed the door in his face. Neha had reached the bottom of the stairs and was walking towards a car. He knew Mourya would stay true to his words and not let him in for the rest of the night and probably kick him.

"Come on, Jane, you can do this. It's just a quick question," he muttered to himself as he walked down the stairs. He reached the bottom before calling out to her as her hand rested on the door, preparing to get into the car. "Neha?"

She turned around, her expression disheartened from earlier, as the conversation they shared probably wasn't what she was expecting at all when she came to speak with him.

"Yes?"

"I.." Jane noticed the other woman in the car, eyeing him suspiciously. Neha followed his gaze before closing the car door.

"Don't worry about her; that's just my sister. Are you alright, Jane?"

"I-I-I was just wondering if you... perhaps if you.. you and I... " He clapped his hand over his face. Why was forming sentences such a struggle? He felt the warmth of her hand touch his hand and pull it back down his face. She had a small smile on her face.

"Take your time, Jane. I'm in no rush. "

Jane took a deep breath several times before looking at her once more. "Would you like to have lunch with me?"

"Lunch?" she repeated.

"Sure, I'd love to."

"I understand I-wait..." His eyes grew weary and he was pretty sure his heart had skipped several beats before her answer registered in his head. "You actually want to go to lunch?"

"Yes, that's what you were asking, right?" She giggled at his shocked expression. "I'm actually off tomorrow if you want to meet up then."

Jane had felt a sense of relief and relaxation wash over him when he heard her laugh.

"Yeah, I have the day off too. We can do it then. I mean, go to lunch. We can go to lunch then. "

"Sounds good. Would you like my number? You can choose the spot where we meet up. "

"Your number? Can I have it? "

"Unless you want to communicate through some other method." I'm afraid I've never been telepathic and the ranger radio is down back at my place. "

She said in a teasing voice, but he didn't hear any of that. He was still focused on the idea that she was willing to give him her phone number.

"No, the phone is fine."

"Alright, I don't have any paper with me... do you?"

He abruptly thrust his hand in her face to signal her that they didn't need a piece of paper, his skin would suffice for the time being. She smirked up at him before jotting down her digits on his palm.

"Let me know," Neha told him with a wink before placing the pen back into her pocket and then opening up the car door once more.

"I-I will."

18

Making Plans

Jane headed back up the stairs, staring at his hand with a wide grin on his face. Since he wasn't paying attention to his surroundings, he ended up walking right into the door, ramming his forehead and nose painfully. His eyes watered from the burning sensation in his nose as Mourya opened up the door.

"Well, did you do it?" There was no time for him to be concerned about Jane's possible injuries because if the man hadn't done what he was told to do, Mourya was only going to be adding to those injuries. "Did you ask her, Jane?"

Jane nodded after wiping his eyes before showing Mourya the numbers written in his palm.

"Oh, my baby boy!" Mourya said, throwing the door open and pulling Jane into a big hug, nearly lifting the other man off the floor.

"Easy, easy," Jane squeaked out before he was placed back down.

"See, I bet it wasn't as bad as you thought it was going to be. This is why you need to listen to me more often. I am the epitome of wisdom. I am guided. "

"Now where should I invite her to lunch? What are we even going to talk about? I have to sit at a table with her and talk with her. "

"Yes, that's normally how these things work, Jane," Mourya sighed, "and you can talk about anything you want to; talk about puppies and rainbows, oooh unicorns, women like those sorts of things."

Jane gave him a look. "Have you actually held a discussion with a woman about rainbows and unicorns?"

"Well, no, but that's because the women I talk to aren't talkers — they're doers. LOL"

Jane scrunched up his face before pushing his way past Mourya and heading to the living room.

"This is the perfect time for you to just ask her questions. The first date is all about getting to know someone. Their likes and dislikes. "

"Date? N-no, this isn't a date... is it?"

"You asked her to lunch. What did you think it was?"

"I ask you to go to lunch all the time. That doesn't make it a date."

"Yes, but you don't fancy me in those respects, at least, I hope not. Jane, I only like you as a friend. You've always been like a brother to me. But back to the original topic, this is a date. She gave you her number, she came all the way out here to speak with you, and that only lasted for five minutes. Call me crazy, but I think she likes you too, Jane. But you have to give it a shot. "

Jane sat down on the couch, grabbing a pillow and burying his face in it with a frustrated scream.

"Seriously, look at me!" Mourya walked over to the place, his hands on Jane's shoulders as the man dropped the pillow. "Look at me, Jane! This isn't as complicated as your mind is making it out to be. You just have to ask her simple questions and listen. Ask her what she does for work? Ask her what her favourite colour is. Ask her what her favourite food is... actually ask her that right now! "

"What?"

"Text her. Ask her what her favourite food is... this way we can figure out where you'll be eating lunch tomorrow. "

"Alright, yeah, I can do that." Jane slipped his phone out of his pocket and carefully added Neha's number before attempting to text her. But his fingers shook violently to the point where he couldn't even hold his phone steady. By the time he finished the text, it made absolutely no sense.

"What the hell is that?" Mourya pointed to the jumbled letters.

"I can't do this! I can't do this! " Jane threw his phone away from him.

"Fine, I'll do it for you!"

Watching as Mourya skipped across the way, the man scooped up the phone and began texting away while reading what he wrote out loud.

"Hello. It's Jane. I was just wondering what sort of food do you enjoy?"

"And now we wait!" Mourya said, sitting down next to Jane on the couch. A couple of minutes later, the cell phone vibrated, signalling the incoming text.

"What did she say?" Jane whispered as he continued to hide behind his pillow.

"She said, she's really not picky. Ugh! " Mourya rolled his eyes. "I hate it when women say that. I'm not picky, but then you bring 'em to a place and all they do is complain the entire time. Or when they say, Oh, I'm not hungry, but then there they are picking off your plate..."

Jane stared at him blankly for a moment. "Do you mind? Can we focus on the task at hand here? Then afterward you can rant all you want about women eating off your plate. "

"Fine...I dunno...um."

"What about Marionette's?" Jane suggested

"Don't you think that place is at all creepy?" "All the puppets around and stuff?"

"It's quirky, sure, but she'll remember the first date for the rest of her life, won't she?"

"Alright, it's your date."

"Good. Go ahead and send her the address to it now. "

"Now that that is settled, let's move on. You know what else I can't stand? "

Jane sighed as he leaned back into the sofa after finishing his text. "What?"

"When a woman asks how she looks in something but good or fantastic, isn't the answer? They want specifics! "

"This is going to be a long night." Jane groaned.

"I have no idea what colour goes best with your dang shoes!"

"So where did you agree to meet him up tomorrow?" Sasha asked as the two sisters sat on the couch eating their dinner.

"He said some place called Marionette's." Neha answered before shoving a forkful of chicken into her mouth.

"Oh no!" Sasha shook her head.

"What?"

"That place is weird."

"Why?"

"Because there are puppets all over the place!" Sasha shivered.

"Aww, come on Sasha, you used to love puppets when you were younger, remember? Did Dad usually put on a show for us around bedtime? Make them dance all over the place. "

Sasha smirked. "Yeah, I remember those. I remember him doing all the crazy little voices. "

"The mom would come in saying..."

"Keep it down. What are the neighbours going to think?" "The two said together before bursting into giggles."

Once the laughter died down, Neha sighed, placing her food down. "I still miss him like crazy."

"I know," Sasha said, "So do I."

"I just felt like he made things so much simpler for all of us. He just kept everything together."

"Yeah, he did. He was good at that; he always kept a smile on his face even when things weren't going well. "

The two fell silent.

"You know," Sasha started after a few moments, "We should see mom at some point and have that brunch with her that she's been wanting. I can only imagine how lonely she is around the house some days. "

"Yeah, you're right. I'll go... as long as my health isn't brought up in the conversation. "

"Deal. Besides, you can tell her all about your creepy puppet lunch. "

19

Hello Puppet

"All right, my friend," Mourya said, standing back and admiring all of his efforts to make Jane presentable."You look great."

He spun Jane around so the man could get a good look at himself in the mirror. He expected Jane's face to light up and for him to be pleased with his new look. However, it was not the reaction that he expected as Jane looked struck with horror.

"I look like I should be in the movies Grease!" The man cried out as he pulled at his attire, which consisted of a leather jacket. Whatever had possessed Mourya to think that he could feel comfortable in such clothing was beyond him.

"Hey!" Mourya snapped, turning to face Jane. "Matt Damon looked pretty good in that movie."

The two exchanged silent looks for a moment before Mourya cleared his throat and looked away first.

"I'm going to go rinse out whatever it is that you put into my hair and I'm going to put on clothes that do not fully consist of leather," Jane told him as he removed the jacket. "I'm going on a date with a pretty girl, not a biker gang."

"They dig the leather! Fine, you know what, go ahead and change, but I'm telling you, it was a good look. "

"Sure."

After washing out the gel and spray gunk from his scalp, Jane dried his hair and slipped on a t-shirt. He walked back out to the kitchen to see Mourya sitting there with a pout on his lips and his arms folded over his chest. He looked like a child that had been informed that he wasn't getting any dessert for his bad behaviour. For a moment, Jane felt bad because he knew that Mourya meant well when it came to trying to help him out. He knew that he had to be thankful to Mourya for helping him because, without his friend, he would have been a nervous wreck before the date was set to begin.

Jane called out to Mourya, "I'm going to keep the jacket on if it makes you feel any better." Mourya frowned, instantly replacing the frown on his face with a happy grin.

"Good, it makes you look like a bada** and girls love that type," Mourya said.

"Yes, because from all the times that I have literally choked on my words and cowered in a corner, Neha is fully aware that I'm a complete and total baddie."

"Well, when you put it like that."

Jane shook his head. "Alright," he said, with a deep breath, "I can do this."

"Yes, you can. You two are going to have a great time, surrounded by creepy as puppets. "

Jane glared at him. "Thanks, that was the boost of confidence I needed."

"Go!" Mourya laughed before directing him out of the flat. "Don't start second-guessing anything. You're only going to end up keeping the lady waiting. Who knows what could happen to her when you're not around. "

"That's not funny, Mourya at all. It's a serious condition and she could die."

Jane nodded and went to open the door when Mourya started singing.

Waiting outside the small restaurant with his hands in the pockets of his jeans, Jane glanced up at the sign that read Marionette's. There was a menacing little puppet painted with eyes that seemed to just look through anyone's soul, making him regret the choice to choose the restaurant.

"Good choice, Janc," he scolded himself. "Brave freaking choice."

He pulled his hands from his pockets and rubbed them over his face as he let out a heavy sigh. He couldn't help but feel completely stupid for bringing

Neha to such a place. It was incredibly creepy and he was trying to make a better impression, but so far he was failing again.

"Jane!"

His head shot up as he saw Neha crossing the street, waving in his direction.

"Hi!" He quickly raised his hand to wave, but slowly brought it back down to his side. He didn't want to appear overly excited. Mourya had warned him it would come across as too strong. She smiled as she neared him, making sure to be quite careful of the curb as she hopped over it to stand next to him. "

"I'm glad my GPS didn't decide to screw me over again," she said.

"Did you drive here?" he asked, glancing around as he tried to figure out which direction she had come from.

"Actually no, I'm not allowed to drive." She replied with an embarrassed expression. Jane's face became grave as he watched her turn red.

"I, uh, took the train," Neha told him as she looked down at her feet. "Sorry, if I'm late."

"No, no! I just didn't know you were going to have to take the train. I would have chosen a place close to you—"

"No..." Neha shook her. "Please, I really like taking the train."

"Do you?"

She nodded. "This gives me some sort of freedom since I can't drive anymore."

He knew that his worst fear was for the entire date to be full of awkwardness, and so far, they were off to a rough start, mainly because he was asking all the wrong questions, He decided to ask one that he knew wouldn't screw things up.

"Would you like to head inside?" Jane questioned. "I-I... I hope this place will suffice."

"It looks lovely," Neha said, looking through the window. "When you said Marionette's, I was quite confused. I had never heard of the place, but my sister has been here."

"And?"

"She said it was creepy."

Jane felt like he was going to be sick.

"But I really like puppets," she added.

"Y-y-you do?"

"Yes, is that weird? Oh God, that does sound incredibly weird out loud. " She turned away from him. "Please forget that I said that."

Jane smirked. "I will once go inside," he said, opening the door. The more he was around her, the more he could finally feel his confidence building, especially since she seemed just as nervous. It was nice to know that he wasn't alone with the rattled nerves.

Inside, there were marionette puppets all over the restaurant. Some hung from the ceiling, others were propped up in little displays near the booths where people could sit. While Jane regretted his choice of place, Neha didn't seem bothered by them at all. He watched as she lifted her hand and touched one of the puppets lightly.

"My dad had a whole set of puppets similar to these when I was younger. He would put shows on for my sister and me all the time."

"That sounds fun."

Neha shrugged. "It was a lot of fun. He was a lot of fun."

"Mmmm, I've wanted to talk to you for a long time!"

And now you are officially creepier than the puppets. Bravo, Jane thought to himself.

"But you didn't because..."

"Because I was nervous."

"Nervous of me? I don't bite," she chuckled.

"No, I know that." Jane blushed, scratching the back of his head.

"But... you... you're... you're p-p-perfect."

20

The Definition of Perfect

Neha nearly choked as Jane uttered out the last part, thankful that she wasn't drinking anything as of yet, or she probably would have turned into a human sprinkler. Her throat burned from her nervous reaction, leaving an unpleasant look on her face as she glanced up at him.

"Oh, Jane..." she said gently, after clearing her throat, "I'm nowhere near perfect. Believe me when I say that."

"I can't," Jane told her, "because it's what I believe. I think everything about you is perfect."

"I... I." It was Neha's turn to be completely lost for words as she stared at the handsome man seated across from her. A small smile played on his lips as she focused his attention outside the window.

"I'm sorry," he said, "It wasn't my intention to make you feel uncomfortable. I just had to put that out there. I'm sure you hear it a lot."

"No," Neha said, confused, "No one has ever called me perfect and, to be honest, I'm not sure how to react to it. I mean, I'm flattered, don't get me wrong. But I don't think I can live up to the status of perfection. "

"That's because the idea of perfection that you have and the idea of perfection that I have are quite different."

"Wh-What do you mean?"

"When I think of people, I think about all the qualities that make that person perfect. From their laugh to the way they focus so incredibly hard on a Sudoku puzzle that they know they are terrible at."

Neha broke into a smile before she started laughing in her seat.

"And what do you think of when you hear perfect? All those women that are glamoured and televised?"

She could only find herself nodding to this question.

"No," Jane said, "those people aren't the universal definition of perfect. And do you know why?"

The entire time he spoke, he refused to look at her fully, only catching her movements from the corner of his eye. He saw her shake her head in response.

"Because there is no universal definition of perfect, perfection is different in everyone's eyes. What one person may see as perfect, another might view as flawed. Just like now, I believe you are perfect, but all you can think of is your flaws."

Neha rubbed her hands together as they settled into her lap. She didn't want to come across as uncomfortable, but receiving such praise just rendered her speechless for a short amount of time. It was certainly flattering, but she just couldn't bring herself to see it as true.

"Are you basing this so-called perfection solely on the outward appearance, though?" Neha asked him. "We've hardly said much to each other, how would you be able to witness any of my flaws?"

"No, I don't base it on your appearance. I based it on the things I've seen you do. How do you go to work every day even after getting yelled at on the phone for a good time. That shows me you are strong. The way you took the train here because you didn't want anyone to drive you, shows that you are quite independent. How you had a seizure aboard the train and still insisted on taking the train... I admire all those traits because I don't think I could ever do all that. And that's why I think you're perfect."

He suddenly laughed. "I think that just makes me sound incredibly stubborn."

"Your flaws are what make you perfect." Jane said.

"I'm afraid I don't follow."

"Your flaws make you perfect because of how you handle them. You don't let them define you, you work through them, and that's amazing."

Jane took a deep breath and exhaled, trying to slow his heart rate which was accelerating every time he looked over at Neha.

"And what about you?" she said.

"What about me?"

"You don't see yourself as perfect? Do you?"

"Me?" he pointed to himself. "Oh no... not at all."

"Do you think someone views you as perfect?"

"I don't see how they could," Jane said. "I have too many flaws that I can't get past. I can hardly function properly on my own."

Neha rested her chin in her hands as she leaned her elbow on the table.

"But you come across as the perfect gentleman."

He peered over at her. "I do?"

"Yes. The way you helped me on the train and left a note-"

He grimaced at the mention of the note.

"It was an incredibly sweet thing to do," she said, catching on to his facial expression. "I imagine it was quite stressful for those around me in the state. I apologise if I got any drool on you during the entire thing. I've been known to do that in the past. My sister makes a big fuss about it sometimes, but not as much as my mother."

"I wouldn't have cared, I think there were a lot more things that were of higher concern than getting a little bit of spit on myself. That shouldn't be anyone's concern during a moment like that."

"And that's what makes you a gentleman," she said, "also, the way you tried to help with the puzzle without trying to help me completely."

"I figured it's something that you want to do on your own. You work on them every morning since I've seen you. And as angry as you got with them, you continued with them. I assured you you were just trying to challenge yourself."

"You noticed all that?"

"I noticed a lot of things about you, Neha, I noticed, not to sound like a complete creep."

"No, it doesn't sound creepy at all."

He averted his gaze from his silverware as he continued to speak with her.

He was running his hands over the napkin to keep his hands from shaking terribly in front of her. As long as he kept his senses busy, he wouldn't feel overwhelmed.

"It was just incredibly hard to focus on anything else once you started taking the train."

Neha was sure her face was terribly red from all the flattering and sweet things he was saying. All the while, he appeared so shy, almost afraid that she would become offended by the things he told her.

"I wish you would have approached me sooner, Jane," she said honestly.

"I didn't think you wanted to be bothered."

"I don't think I would have found myself bothered by you in any way."

Jane hid his smile behind his hands before Neha reached across the way and pulled it down softly.

"Don't hide your smile, Jane."

Jane looked at the hand that she touched, his skin tingling under the warmth of her hand. Suddenly, he found himself pulling his hand away dropping his hands to his side.

"I'm sorry," Neha began, but Jane quickly interjected.

"No, it's not you. Don't be sorry. I just... if you haven't noticed Neha, I'm a bit of a mess."

"You're not a mess, Jane."

"Yes, I am. My anxiety deters me from doing so much. I can hardly look you in the eye right now, and all we're doing is talking."

Neha watched as his thumb ran circles in the centre of his opposite hand.

"And before you couldn't find yourself to talk to me," she pointed out with a small smile, "which means you are making quite a large stride, don't you think?"

21

Red

Jane glanced up from his meal that consisted of a simple salad and looked at Neha, who had been aimlessly stirring her soup for the last fifteen minutes as she looked out the window. They hadn't spoken a word since the waiter arrived with their meals, partially because neither of them was sure what to discuss. What were the chances that the two worst people when it came to small talk had found themselves sharing lunch together? The waiter had come over repeatedly, wondering if something was wrong with the food, as they weren't talking at all. But they reassured him each time that the food was fine. They were just socially impaired.

"What's your favourite color?" he asked her, suddenly drawing her attention back in from the little bird that was hopping about on the sidewalk outside.

"My favourite color?" She repeated, "Um... uh.. Purple, I think."

"You think, you don't know your favourite color?" Jane said curiously.

"Well, some people say that as adults, it's impossible to have a favourite color. That it's only a thing in childhood that we grow out of. To be honest, I also like black. It's hard for me to choose a favourite since it varies from day to day. I like purple today because I thought my purple blouse would go well with these pants. " She admitted. "What about you? What's your favourite color? "

"Red," he answered. "It's always been red."

"Why red?"

The colour red is one of my favorites.Apples, strawberries, Clifford the Big Red Dog... did you read those books as a kid?"

Neha grinned. "I did. I quite liked the idea of having a rather large dog to ride around the neighbourhood with. Of course, it turned out that the majority of my family is allergic to dogs."

"Really? And you're not allergic? "

"Not in the slightest."

"Well, why not get a dog now?"

"Because I live with my sister as of now," Neha sighed, "which means no dog. Maybe one day, though. Although, I don't think my mother and sister are going to let me move out of Sasha's apartment, anytime soon."

"Why is that? Because of the..." Jane stopped himself, feeling as though even mentioning her condition was taboo.

Neha seemed to understand his hesitation. "Because of the seizures? Yes. You don't have to tiptoe around the subject, Jane, I'm not offended when people say seizure or epilepsy. It's just part of who I am. It's not like it's a dirty swear."

"Sorry, I just never met someone who... who had epilepsy. I wasn't sure what was appropriate to say."

"It's okay," Neha reassured him. "I've grown up with it, so nothing really bothers me anymore when it comes to questions, I'm hardly phased because no one has really asked me anything new about it over the years.

"From medication to how it affects my sex drive"

Jane spit his water onto the table, allowing some to dribble down his chin and onto his shirt as he quickly reached for a napkin. Neha couldn't help but laugh as she covered one hand over her mouth to hide her smile.

"People actually ask you that?" he asked her, once he had cleared up his mess. She nodded her head before leaning forward on the table.

"People have absolutely no shame sometimes, Jane. They don't care if it makes you uncomfortable, just as long as someone answers their questions. I don't really care anymore, but you should have seen my face when people used to ask such things. "

"Is it scary?" Jane inquired, his curiosity getting the best of him at the moment, "the seizures, I mean, not the people. Although I can imagine that some people who have approached you with such questions must be somewhat scary."

"I'm only scared when I wake up," she said, "and that's because I'm not sure what happened during the time that I was out like during the accident. One moment, I'm driving... next thing I know, my car is totaled and wrapped around a tree."

Neha saw the look of horror sweep across his face as he listened. "I..I.. I'm so sorry, Neha. I had no idea. I didn't know."

"Well, how could you?" She said, with a calm smile, "I hadn't told you until now."

"So this is why you take the train?"

"Yeah, I don't trust myself behind the wheel anymore. Plus, they took my licence after that. I have to go a full year with no seizures before they'll even consider it again. That was the condition last time, but I'm not sure they'll let me get behind the wheel again."

"I can imagine it was quite traumatizing."

"I guess what really worried me when I awoke was that... well, I wasn't sure if I had hurt anybody. I couldn't imagine the thought of losing control of the wheel and crashing into somebody. Fortunately, it didn't happen and the tree was more than forgiven. "

"Anyways, enough about me, Jane. What about you?"

"ME?"

"Yes, you. You hardly talk about yourself... It's not a bad thing to be humble, but I'd like to know things about you as well. I feel like you know me pretty well... better than most of my co-workers, and I've known them forever. "

"I'm afraid there's nothing really special about me, Neha." He said, pressing himself to the corner of the booth.

"Of course there is."

"No, there really isn't anything. I am the only child of a bitter man and a woman who walked out on his family long ago. I worked for my father until only yesterday when he decided to fire me for being tardy. So needless to say, I don't have a healthy relationship with my family."

Neha sat in silence as he turned away. The conversation had taken a dark turn. She pushed her hair back before standing up and leaving her seat.

Jane could hear her standing up and prepared himself to face the fact that she was leaving the date because he had ruined it. But instead, he felt someone was sitting next to him. He craned his neck over his shoulder and saw Neha take the spot beside him.

"You are far too hard on yourself, Jane. There's no need to speak so ill. "

"I speak the truth."

"Perhaps. But not once did you mention the fact that you are a kind person who is amazing with numbers, enough so that you could just glance over at my puzzle and instantly know that I was wrong. A person who helped a random stranger on a train and is very witty and funny. All the positive attributes that you failed to mention. "

"But-"

"But nothing, Jane. Be kinder to yourself; you deserve it."

22

That Guy

As Jane wandered into the apartment later that day after his date with Neha, Mourya glanced over the back of the sofa to see a dreamy look on the man's face as well as a smile as he headed to his bedroom without a word.

"It must have been a pretty good date." "Hell, I don't even look like that when I come home the morning after," Mourya chuckled to himself before focusing back on the game. He would wait until Jane was ready to disclose the details of what had taken place during the lucheon.

Jane laid down on his bed and let out a happy sigh as his hand touched the side of his face where Neha had given him a departing kiss. It had been completely unexpected, and yet Jane had to control himself from squealing out in delight. That would have come across as pathetic if he had actually done it.

But before she left to take the train home, she agreed to meet up again and said they would discuss it on the train. He was thrilled at the idea that he didn't feel so entirely nervous about talking to her as much. Talking to her for hours at the puppet restaurant had been enough for Jane to be somewhat comfortable around her. Especially after all that was said between them.

Then it hit him, like a punch to the throat, leaving him deprived of air for a few moments.

He wouldn't be taking the train; he no longer needed to as he didn't work at his father's firm anymore. It had apparently slipped Neha's mind as well, as she thought she was going to see him riding the train to work.

He yanked his pillow from under his head and placed it over his face, letting out a frustrated yell that startled Mourya in the living room. Several seconds later, his roommate appeared with a frying pan and a knife in hand, standing in the doorway.

"Mourya, what the hell are you doing with the knife and a frying pan?" Jane cried out, falling off his bed.

"What the hell are you doing screaming like you're possessed!? I almost ran out of sofa.You nearly scared the living daylights out of me!These things aren't cute, Jane! You can't do that to me! "

Neha was walking down the sidewalk to the apartment after leaving the train station, a never fading smile on her face since she left Jane at the restaurant to catch a train back home. She couldn't wait to tell Sasha all about it. Perhaps then her sister would feel better about the whole ordeal.

She grabbed her keys from the pocket of her coat and looked up only to see Arjun waiting outside on the steps. She groaned, debating whether or not she should turn back around and try to avoid him.

"Neha!" he called to her.

Apparently, it was too late.

With a polite smile on her face, she walked over. He greeted her with a hug, drawing her into his chest. She cleared her throat before finally making her way out of his grasp.

"Hello Arjun, How have you been?" She asked, smoothing the front of her coat with her hands to avoid his gaze.

"So formal now," he chuckled. "Where have you been?"

Neha stared down at an existing crack in the sidewalk. "I was at lunch," she told him before looking up. She saw his face drop. He didn't look pleased with her at all.

"So what Sasha said is true then?" His hands came to rest on her shoulders as his face twisted with bitterness. "You were out on a date?"

"Wh-what? No, I was meeting up with the gentleman that helped me out on the train and-"

"And what?" he said hotly. "What did you two end up doing?"

Neha took a step back but kept her chin up. "It's none of your business what we did. But if you must know, we went to a small place and ate food just like any normal person would if they went to a restaurant. "

"And do you like him?"

"What does it matter to you, Arjun?" She huffed as she walked up a couple of the stairs, only to be stopped by the man again as he ran up the steps and blocked her from continuing on.

"It hasn't been that long since you stopped talking to me, Neha. I can't believe-"

"Hold up!" She placed her hand up in his face, silencing him. "You dare bring that up? If you want to say it hasn't been that long, but according to a lot of people, it didn't take you long to get under someone else."

Arjun's face paled slightly.

"Let me get this clear..." A mocking laugh escaped her throat as she looked up for a moment in disbelief.

"Because of that man? Were you seeing him earlier than just today, Neha? Be honest."

"And now you're accusing me, good lord, Arjun. Get some help. "

"And what's that?"

"I don't want to forget about that guy. Because he's not just some guy. He's.."

"He's what?" Arjun asked with an eye roll. However, he stopped when he noticed the bright smile on Neha's face as she looked away from him, seemingly staring off into the distance as she reminisced about the lunch she had that afternoon. Finally, she looked back at him, looking as happy as ever.

"He's perfect."

23

Something is Missing

Neha boarded the train on her way to work one morning and glanced around. How different the train felt without Jane's presence, even though she had only recently discovered that they actually took the train together.

She felt a slight guilt for being so blind to the man who knew so much about her just from observation. Sasha and others found it creepy, but it wasn't like he was keeping a journal about her, he was simply observing so he could find something to talk to her about. His problem was that he just couldn't bring himself to actually speak to her for so long.

When Jane informed her that he wouldn't be taking the train anymore because he didn't work there anymore, she felt a sense of sadness, wishing that perhaps she could go back in time and notice the man who noticed her out of the crowd that took the train each morning.

She didn't know Jane that well yet. But she planned on getting to know the man more. There was something about Jane's shyness and humility that was so refreshing to Neha that she almost couldn't stand it.

Since their lunch date, they hadn't spoken all that much and Neha figured it was because Jane didn't know how to start a conversation and it normally resulted in him texting out a random question, like what was her favourite movie or if she had been to Australia.

She had to admit, she was no better at starting conversations either. Most of the time, she was so used to talking about her work that her conversation skills were completely lacking with all those that weren't part of her inner circle.

Despite their awkward and short conversations, they managed to arrange a second meet-up. This time, it was up to Neha to figure out what they were going to do.

Sitting at his home when he would normally be on the train, Jane wasn't sure what to do with himself as he found himself rolling an orange back and forth on the kitchen table for a source of entertainment. Although he wasn't entertained in the slightest, he was occupied for the time being.

"You're so weird," Mourya said as he walked into the kitchen, buttoning up his shirt as he was dressed for work.

"How am I weird?" Jane questioned him, the orange nearly rolling off the table before he leaned forward and snatched it up. He held it close to him while Mourya gave him an odd stare.

"What are you doing with the orange?" he asked.

Jane glanced down and quickly placed it back in the fruit bowl.

"I'm not really sure. I'm just... bored. I've been bored since I woke up and realised that I had nothing to do. I never thought I would miss work so much. "

"Well, you don't miss that job, but you probably miss having something to do."

"I guess so. I need to get another job. "

"Jane, why don't you take just a small vacation for now? You need to relax for a bit. You'll be fine not working for a while. You've got enough money saved up to take a trip around the world if you wanted to. You don't need to work."

"Then what am I supposed to do then?"

"I dunno. You can do what I do."

"And that is?"

"Watch some television, drink a bit, reminisce about the good ol'days and... nap. Take lots of naps."

"That doesn't sound fun at all," Jane frowned. He wasn't much of a sleeper to begin with, and normally, he found it very difficult to nap during the day. On the days that he actually tried, he found himself waking up with a terrible headache.

"Don't knock it until you try it," Mourya said before leaving towards the door. "For once in your life, be lazy! You just might like it! "

Jane was left alone, and after sitting in the kitchen for a few minutes, he arose and left to enter the living room to watch some television.

During the day, there wasn't much on that he wanted to watch.

He didn't like drinking, so he settled for a glass of water.

There wasn't much to reminisce about for him.

And he didn't feel tired at all enough to nap.

"How does Mourya do this daily?" he questioned to himself.

He glanced down at his phone that rested on the coffee table, and he debated whether he should text Neha and see how her day was going. He felt terrible for not being the greatest at conversation in person or via text.

He needed to try harder.

However, once again, his mind got in the way as he started to question if he should message her in the first place. He knew that she was at work, and he didn't want to interrupt her. But from how she described her boss, perhaps messaging her would brighten her day just a little bit. At least that's what he was hoping for.

Neha rubbled her eyes after staring at a rough manuscript for the last three hours. The words were all beginning to merge and her eyes burned something fierce. Her eyelids felt as though they were being weighed down by bricks, making it harder to keep her eyes open as they threatened to close. She wasn't even halfway through her day and already the girl was about ready to fall asleep at her desk when her cellphone went off beside her. She glanced around her to make sure Mr. Daniel wasn't making his rounds before opening up the text.

"I hope your day is going well. I'm stuck at home, not sure what to do with myself."

She smiled, suddenly feeling wide awake before she replied.

"I'm willing to trade places. Mind editing for several hours at a time?"

She set her phone aside and went to return to her work, but only seconds later did she get a reply.

"I think I'll pass on that. It's hard for me to find something I enjoy reading. "

Oh no, Neha thought to herself, that was unacceptable. She loved reading and hearing that someone was unable to find suitable reading material made her smile. "Oh no, that would never do. She knew that anyone could enjoy a book as long as they found the right one. If a person found a book worth reading, they would certainly change their minds about not being much of a reader.

She smiled as she figured out where they would go for their second adventure.

24

Thriller

Neha waited patiently outside for Jane to arrive as she fixed her clothing to make sure it didn't look like she had just rolled out of bed... even though she had. It had been a long night for her as she felt sick from her medication, but she kept it to herself as she turned in for the night, wishing Sasha sweet dreams. Fortunately, nothing happened through the hours as she tossed and turned, as the medicine seemed to do somewhat of its job, but it left her feeling groggy the morning after as she sat on her bed for several minutes trying to collect herself. Finally, she had motivated herself enough to get out of bed and grab some clothing from the closet.

Sasha had asked numerous times throughout the morning if she was feeling up to it. If Neha had any sort of notion that she wasn't feeling well, her sister wouldn't let her out of the home. She reassured her plenty of times before she left that she was just fine and if she needed anything she would call.

The unsettling churning of her abdomen caused goosebumps to rise on her arms, trailing down her spine to her legs. Her hands touched the cell phone in her pocket as she thought about calling it all off. She felt her stomach turn in knots. Normally that meant the worse was to come sooner or later in the day, and she really hoped, like other times, that it was just a false alarm. She didn't want the day to be ruined, nor did she want Jane to witness her having another seizure.

It was embarrassing to even have her family witness it. She was never fully certain of what happened when she lost consciousness, but she never dared to ask either. She had seen some of what occurred from the videos that her mother and Sasha had shown doctors in the past and from what Neha had witnessed. It was probably for the best that she wasn't fully aware of all her actions during that time.

She decided to sit down on the cement stairs as she felt slightly light-headed.

"Please," she begged with her body as she rested her head against her hands, "not today."

"Hello." Jane's quiet voice pulled her out of her prayer stance as she looked over to him. She flashed him a smile as he walked over and sat down beside her.

"I was hoping I went to the right spot," he said, glancing back at the building behind them.

"This is the spot," she said, forcing out a cheery tone.

"So the library, huh?" Jane said, nodding his head. "I'm guessing this has to do with what I told you the other day."

She nodded. "When you told me you couldn't find anything good to read, I knew I had to change that right away." She chuckled.

"So we're going to find a book?"

"Yes. That's the challenge of the day! Come on." She pushed herself up and quickly regretted moving so fast as she got a sense of dizziness.

"Are you alright?" Jane asked her.

"Who me? Yeah, I'm fine," she said before leading the way inside.

Jane didn't seem so convinced but didn't want to argue with her as he followed her inside.

The two were greeted by the warmth of the library as the cooler months were settling in, leaving it extremely chilly outside. It was quite as one would expect a library to be, with people sitting in different sections. Some were on computers, others were surrounded by books on the tables they occupied.

"Alright," Neha said in a low voice after clapping her hands together lightly, "what sort of things do you like, action and adventure?"

"Er... not really. I won't watch an action movie unless Mourya forces me to."

He made a face that meant to. She giggled. "Okay, how about historical? Fiction or non-fiction?"

"I was terrible at history; I had a hard time remembering dates and events."

"Well, you told me you liked Clifford the Big Red Dog books," she joked, "maybe we should venture to the kid section?"

Jane smirked as he scratched the back of his neck. "I don't think parents would look so kindly on a man standing in the kid's section of the library. They might get the wrong impression."

"I suppose you're right about that. Well..." she placed her hands on her hips and glanced around.

"What do you like to read?" Jane asked her. "Romance?" he guessed.

"Oh no... I will leave that to my mother and sister. They could read and watch romance stories all day every day. That's why they have all these unrealistic expectations... that and Disney movies. "

"You are not a fan of Disney?"

"Now I didn't say that. But I prefer movies where it isn't centred around love all the time. Like Mulan, that was a good movie. The sequel... not so much."

"I didn't even know there was a sequel."

"Just pretend there isn't one," she advised. "My favourite genre is mystery and thriller. Psychological thrillers keep me reading into the night, but I have no regrets in the morning. Those are my favourite ones. That's why I became an editor. I always love looking at all the fresh reads that are coming in, and whenever we get a new thriller, I am the first to jump on it and claim it as mine. "

"I think something like that would interest me."

"Yeah? Well then let's go on over to that section and we'll see what we can find. "

She led him down one of the rows and told him to scout for a book while she looked around herself. Her headache was getting worse, and she was trying to mask the pain with a smile anytime Jane looked at her.

Jane wasn't sure what seemed different about Neha that day, but he knew something was up with the girl. No matter how much she smiled, he could see something in her eyes. She looked worried about something, but whenever he asked, she would wave it off as if nothing were wrong. It was familiar to him because it was something he often did when people asked him what was wrong. He didn't want people to discuss business, especially when it was personal. He had to assume that Neha was the same way. He watched her stop several times and touched her head several times, mumbling to herself.

"Find anything yet?" She asked him at one point.

"No, no yet. But maybe we could sit down for a little bit. " He tried to offer her an opportunity to rest if she wasn't feeling well, but she refused as she shook her head back and forth.

"No, no resting," Neha said, "keep looking, we're not leaving here until you find something."

"I'm looking!" he promised. She left the row he was in as Jane read the summaries on the backs of several books. Nothing really tickles his fancy. It was hard for him to find something to read, as he never really enjoyed reading much as a child. He had struggled to learn when he was young, and his father was ruthless, especially when Jane stuttered or stammered over a word.

He could remember the long nights where his father would force him to read aloud, and if he screwed up a word, he had to start from the very beginning of the book. Whenever he was in school and the teacher called upon him to read, he began shaking, terrified that the other students would ridicule something about his reading skills.

But that was all in the past, and reading was obviously something very important to Neha, so he decided to check the next row of books, hoping to find something so Neha wouldn't feel bad about him not reading.

However, as he rounded the corner, he saw Neha sitting at the end of the aisle, her legs stretched out and her head leaned back.

"Neha?"

25

Read All about It

"Neha?! Oh my God. " Jane was washed over with panic as he made his way over and knelt down beside the woman. Her eyes were closed and it looked as though she was either sleeping or dead. He went to her pulse when she spoke to him in a quiet voice.

"Shh, Jane, it's alright." Neha's voice reminded him of a mother's voice lying to soothe a child after they woke up from a night. She opened her eyes and gave him a small smile as she kept her head tilted back.

"Oh God, I was sure you were having one... one of them."

She shook her head slightly and winced at the movement. "No, I haven't had one yet, but I might." She sighed.

"You might?"

"I've been feeling pretty crappy all day, so it normally means that one is coming my way."

"Should I call for help?"

"No, no, no!" She said, "Pleasc don't. I don't want to be in the hospital again. If I have one, I'm sure it won't be as bad as the other ones. "

"I don't follow."

"Normally, the ones I can feel coming aren't as severe. If I don't have a sign, then it's bad. I've felt it since this morning. "

"If you weren't feeling well, why didn't you tell me?"

"Because I didn't want you to worry," she said, "I know your anxiety could-"

"To hell with my anxiety, Neha!" he replied bluntly. Her eyes widened at his tone.

"I don't care about my anxiety in a situation like this..." Jane informed her. It was true, there were times when his nerves and anxiety disappeared, usually due to an adrenaline rush. "I don't want you to get hurt just because you think I'll freak out. If you weren't feeling well, you should have said something. "

"I know, but I didn't want to say anything and have it be a false alarm."

"A false alarm?"

"Sometimes I can have the symptoms and then nothing will happen," she explained, "it happens more often than not."

"So... there are different types of seizures?"

"Yes." She rested her head back on one of the shelves. Jane carefully sat down beside her, allowing her to lean against his body if she needed any extra support.

"Each of them varies... sometimes you probably wouldn't be able to tell if someone is having one. It could look like they are daydreaming. That's how mine started when I was younger. I would just go blank out of nowhere. I scared the hell out of my parents after they realised that I wasn't just flat out ignoring them on purpose."

"I bet."

"The onset of them was so long, and then they were so frequently I was put on some strong medication as a kid. My dad didn't really like it. He told me he didn't want things so strong hitting my young system, but it was the only thing that helped me manage them.

"I-" Jane stopped as he felt Neha's hand stiffen in his. He turned his body to face her and felt up her arm as it seemed her entire right side had become tense.

"Okay... okay." Neha breathed slowly, as her eyes were open, looking straight out. Like she had mentioned before, it seemed she had fallen into a daydream as she didn't look panicked, just incredibly stiff.The worry on his face made her feel so guilty for putting him through it. She tried to move to stand up, despite not feeling her strongest in that moment.

"Do you think it's best to stand up?" Jane asked, quickly rising to her feet to assist her. He didn't like the stubbornness of the woman trying to push herself when he figured she should be trying to take it easy. "Are you sure you don't-"

"Jane," Neha cut him off, "Really, it's okay. I don't need to go see a doctor every time I have one. If that was the case, I would pretty much just take up residence in a hospital. "

Jane sighed, rubbing his forehead as he frowned looking at her, but he could see her eyeing his expression. She obviously wasn't going to feel any better if he just continued focusing on it. She was obviously trying to keep moving on with her day.

"I can't believe you can remain so calm during that. Teach me your ways." I joked trying to make light of the situation.

"Years of practice?" she said with a small shrug. "That's the best thing I can come up with. I used to be afraid of them when they first started. I would come to and I would just start freaking out until my parents could calm me down and reassure me that everything was okay. "

"Well..." Jane wasn't sure how to respond, but a small grin appeared on his face when he thought of something. "I think I know what book I'm going to pick up today."

"Really?! Which one? "

Neha couldn't help but blush as they reached out for the checkout desk. The librarian scanned the books, eyeing the selection of books. Jane was practically checking out every single book that explained epilepsy and seizures.

"Did you have to get them all?" she teased as they walked outside.

"Well, I want to know as much as I can about it. If we're going to spend more time together, I'd like to be prepared for anything and everything. That's if you want to spend more time together. I didn't mean to just force myself upon you or anything. We don't have to spend that much time together if you don't want to. I'd never want to pressure you into anything."

He stopped as Neha pulled him into a hug outside the library. The warmth of her body pressed against his.

"Of course I want to spend more time with you."

A/N: Hello everyone. I just wanted to say thank you to all who are reading this book. I didn't expect people to take an interest in it, but I'm so thankful even if you just peeked at it. It's not just a story about love, it's about facing the battles that we don't have a choice to face otherwise. Epilepsy affects at least 65 million people world-wide, and seizures can come in so many forms.

I think it's always great when people take the time to learn how to help someone if they suspect someone is suffering from a seizure. It can save a life.

Also, the book touches on the subject of those that suffer from anxiety disorders. There is no set standard for what occurs when someone experiences an anxiety attack, and it affects people worldwide no matter their age. However, many people are unaware or misinformed when it comes to anxiety, and it often leads to misdiagnoses or people going without proper treatment for too long.

I was hoping to bring awareness to both topics and how they can affect the daily routine of someone's life.

:)

26

More Bad News

When Jane returned to the apartment, he found that Mourya was already home from his work shift and saw the man sitting at the kitchen table. His hands were holding his head up as he continued to run one of them through his shaggy dark hair repeatedly. It wasn't as usual as it was Mourya's normal stance if he was suffering from his hangover.

When Jane entered the kitchen, Mourya peered up at him, a tired expression on his face.

"You don't have your phone on you?" Mourya asked him.

"Uh... yeah... I do... Oh! You know, I turned it off when I went inside the library with Neha. Is everything alright? You look really terrible, Mourya. You really need to take a break from drinking and let your body heal. I keep telling you that stuff is damaging! "

"I wasn't dri-.. wait you went to the library with Neha? What was her idea of a date?"

"Yes," Jane replied, as he could hear that judgemental tone dripping from Mourya's tongue. Mourya wasn't much for libraries, to begin with, and his dates normally consisted of going to the bar and maybe getting something to eat if the woman was lucky enough to get a meal.

"And I had a great time despite her having a seizure in the thriller section."

"She had another one... and in the thriller section of all places?"

"A minor one. She called it partial simple or simple partial... something along those lines. I picked out all these books so I could learn all about it. "

With a loud thud, Jane dropped the books onto the table, bringing Mourya to flinch from the noise, But the man did end up laughing and shaking his head as Jane looked mighty proud of himself in that moment.

"That's dedication, my friend."

It became quite and Jane noticed as Mourya continued to glance up at him and then back down at his hands that were resting on the table, twiddling his thimbs back and forth. He seemed nervous and no matter if he smiled or laughed seconds prior, it returned to a frown. After Mourya let out another sigh, Jane had to ask what was going on with his roommate. If it was a normal hangover, the man would just groan about his headache, grab some coffee and water, and head back to his room.

"Mourya, what's wrong?" "This doesn't look like one of your regular morning hangovers. Are you alright?"

"I don't know how to tell you this, Jane," he began, "because I'm not sure how you're going to react to it."

"Well, keeping it from me is only going to concern me more. So you might as well just tell me. "

Mourya nodded. "You're right. Jane... someone called here earlier looking for you. I guess they tried your cell but when you didn't answer, they called here. "

"Who did it? For what? "

"It was the firm. your father's firm. They were calling because... your dad..."

Mourya's voice continued to trail off, leaving Jane to grow frustrated as he wanted to know what was going on. If it had to do with his father, he assumed it had to be something big as his father wouldn't even call him if he was on fire.

"My father? What about him? Was he calling to apologise for how rotten he's been all these years?"

"Sorry to say, but no. He had his secretary call to inform you that your mother passed away, "Mourya blurted it all out within seconds and quickly looked down to avoid his best friend's gaze.

Jane sat there for a moment, his eyes scanning Mourya's face, hoping it was another of his friend's cruel jokes.

"W-w-what did you say?"

"Your mother passed away last night, Jane. Your father was informed and I was told to tell you. "

Jane covered his face for a few moments, allowing the information to process in his mind before ripping his hands away in anger. "He had his secretary call? He didn't even have the decency to call himself? "

He pushed back his chair as he arose, his face red with anger as the chair fell back and clattered against the floor.

"Jane, I think you're missing the bigger picture here. Dude, your mother-"

"No, I understand my mother is gone. But she was long gone before last night. She left me all those years ago, with him. Not once bothering to check in to see how I was fairing with the monster. All because she was unhappy. If he made her that miserable, what did she expect to do to me? "

Mourya swallowed as his lips curled in a frown. It was the exact reason why he didn't want to be the one to deliver the news; he knew Jane's reaction was not going to be pleasant. The man held a lot of resentment towards his parents for different reasons, and now it was all coming to the surface again. He watched as Jane paced back and forth, shaking his head as he couldn't bring himself to gather his thoughts.

"Now that she's dead, I'm supposed to feel sorrow and sadness for her." "No?"

He left the room, and Mourya listened as the front door slammed, signalling that Jane had left the apartment again.

He wasn't sure what to do with himself as he wondered the streets, hoping an answer would come to him. He hated himself for feeling sad after learning of his mother's death.But he had also come to hate her and his father for different reasons.

He didn't care if they didn't like each other. Plenty of parents in the world were separated and provided healthy and loving homes for their children, but Jane didn't get any of that. He left him to only feel the bitterness of the thoughts of his mother.

The morning she left, she didn't even utter the words. She just walked away, as if he were some stray dog she could dump on someone.That someone turned out to be one of the coldest men Jane had ever met.

After all that was said between Jane and his father, he wished that his father would have a change of heart in a time such as the one they were facing and come to his son directly to inform him of his situation. Instead, the bastard had a secretary call to deliver the news.

What was Jane supposed to do with this newly found information? Was he expected to carry out the funeral proceedings for his mother? A woman he shared no pleasant memories with for as far as he could remember. a woman who wouldn't call to see if Jane was still alive.Now he was supposed to take care of her?

His mind was screaming, his chest was heaving, and all he could do was breakdown and cry. Why couldn't the day end on a positive note? He had left Neha with a smile on both of their faces, and now there he sat on the curb crying in the streets.

His mother was dead.

His father was still a rogue.

The woman he had fallen in love with suffered from a condition that he didn't understand.

And there was no one there at that moment to tell him that everything would be okay.

27

Help is on the Way

The day was growing colder as the sun was starting to set and Jane had yet to venture back into the apartment since receiving the news, no matter how much Mourya begged him. He remained outside, sitting on the curb, staring off into nothing, trying to debate what to do. Of course, it was very much like his father to leave all his troubles on him, as if he really needed any more stress in his life. He found it hard to function enough, and it seemed his father didn't even care that his ex-wife was dead; he was just trying to make it someone else's problem so he didn't have to deal with it.

"It's a bit chilly out here, don't you think?" A voice came out to Jane, causing him to jump and land off the curb and into the street. He quickly turned his head to see Neha approaching as she walked along the sidewalk towards him. She was still wearing the same clothing from when they had met up at the library earlier. Leaving him confused, he saw her get on the train to head home afterward.

"H-how..." he shook his head in disbelief before blinking his eyes several times to make sure he was seeing properly. "What are you doing here, Neha?"

"A little birdie by the name of Mourya rang me up, told me you were upset, so I-"

"You came all the way out here?" He kept trying to push himself up to his feet, but he would only end up rolling over as his thoughts got the best of him, disabling his body momentarily.

"It's not that long of a trip, Jane," Neha said before sitting down next to him on the curb as he finally got himself up enough.

"You shouldn't have come here, Neha. I'm sorry Mourya called you. He shouldn't have."

"And why not? Do you not want my company? "

"No, I mean yes, I want your company, but I didn't want to inconvenience you like that."

"It's not an inconvenience at all. You've helped me out multiple times now, so why can't I help you? " she said.

"I don't think anyone can help me with this mess."

"I'm not fully aware of what the mess is. Mourya just said that he couldn't get you to come inside because you were very upset. You don't have to tell me but..."

"My mother is dead."

Neha gasped before raising her hand to her mouth slightly. Her eyes were wide, scanning over Jane's face before the man looked away from her and focused on his hands. She slowly lowered her hand back down to her side.

"Oh goodness, Jane, I'm sorry."

"Don't be... she was hardly a mother to me, just like how my father was hardly a father," he scoffed. "I'm not even sure what I'm upset about at this point."

She frowned as she wrapped her coat around her small body, tightly scooting close to him.

"How did you find out?"

"My father had his secretary call the house," Jane said bitterly.

"His secretary? Why-"

"Because that's the kind of man he is, Neha. He's a monster, nothing less of a monster. "

"So what does this mean for you?" she pondered curiously.

"I don't know," Jane said honestly. "I really don't know what to make of the entire situation. I can only assume that my father told me so that I could handle all the funeral proceedings. "

"Do you want to handle all that?"

"Ugh. Why should I? " Suddenly, he was up on his feet, pulling at his hair as he paced back and forth on the sidewalk. "She abandoned the idea of me as her son a long time ago, so why should I bother doing what a son would do for his mother?"

Neha didn't say anything for a few moments before she pushed herself up and walked over to him, blocking his pacing path momentarily. "Can anyone else in your family take care of it?"

"No, there is no one else in the family, at least closely related, that would even bother or give a damn that she's dead."

"What happens if no one steps forward for her?"

He let out a heavy sigh. "More than likely, I will end up holding the funeral for her, or at least make sure that her body is taken care of. I don't know why I want to even bother with it... but I can't... I can't just sit there and pretend this didn't happen. I would never be able to forgive myself. I hate both of them, but then I don't and I don't understand why. "

"Answer me this, Jane. If your father approached you right now and asked you to start all over again and make amends, would you?"

Jane bit his lower lip and looked away. "Yes. And that makes me sound incredibly pathetic, I know. "

Neha's hand touched under his chin and gently directed his head to face her.

"You're not pathetic, Jane. You need to stop saying that. Forgiving someone after they've caused you a lifetime of pain, isn't pathetic, it's incredible. You are by far the bigger person in the entire situation. You're one of the strongest people I've come to know because I don't think many people would be able to say the same thing after what you've been through with your father or even with your mother. You know, now that I think about it, this funeral might help you in a way.

"In what way?"

"In a way, this is just a final goodbye between you and your mother. She left you without so much of a word, so you weren't able to say goodbye to her. Now you can. You'll no longer wonder or worry about when she's going to return. This will be her final place, and you'll always know where she is. It'll be a sense of closure for you, at least with her. And maybe one day, you can come to terms with everything and forgive her. "

"Forgive her? Should I forgive her? "

Oh Jane, she doesn't deserve it, she put you through hell. But it's not for her, it's for you. Once you come to terms with forgiving her or at least, letting the past go, I think you'll feel a lot better. Like I said, it doesn't have to be that day or today. But maybe one day."

"I don't know the first thing about holding a funeral or what to even do, Neha."

"Well..." The woman rubbed her foot into the pavement, her eyes focusing on what used to be a bright piece of bubble gum that had eventually become littered with dirt after being stepped on repeatedly. "I can help you out there as much as I can, Jane."

"I don't want to bother."

"Stop," Neha said, covering his mouth with her hands. "You're not bothering anyone. Now let's get you inside, before we both turn into ice. "

28

Voiced Concern

Neha had learned to regret a lot of things in life, such as not spending enough time with her father, but definitely one thing heard the top of the list and that was calling on her mother for help. Normally, when Neha called upon her mother, it would end up as her receiving a lecture about something for some unknown reason. It drove the young girl mad, but there was nothing she really could do unless she wanted to flat out hand upon her mother. Some days she was awfully tempted to do so.

"Mom, all I am asking you to do is to talk to him about what he needs to do during this time," Neha said as she held her cell phone to her ear while claning some dishes in the sink.

"And what exactly do you want me to say, Neha? a funeral is very personal thing, everyone has different wishes and such. Didn't his mother give him last words to sink."

"No, as I already told you about two minutes ago, they didn't get along, they haven't spoken since he was a child. And since his father just kinds threw it all on him, Jane isn't sure what to do. He's overwhelmed with all of this and I jsut want to help him."

"Why do you have to help him, Neha? you have enogh problems of your own..."

Neha pulled the cell phone away from her ear and glared at the screen for a few seconds before she placed it backup. "Enough problems of my own?" She repeated. "Pray tell mother, what are all my problems."

"I didn't mean it to be taken in a hostile tone," her mother began. "What I was trying to say was, you don't need this stress in your life, at all. Not with your condition."

"My condition is manageable. I'm doing fine!"

"Oh really, and when was your last seizure? And don't you dare lie to me. "

Similar to Sasha, her mother often liked looking for some reason to just throw in her face, and it was normally the most recent seizure that they used as leverage. Neha rolled her eyes. "A couple of days ago, but it wasn't even a big one, it was just simple."

"It doesn't matter, Neha. Your condition doesn't seem to be getting any better and I think it's about time that you go back to the doctor and inform them of what's going on so they can help you. You don't need this boy's stress added to your shoulder. "

"He is not stressing me out!" Neha finally yelled, losing her temper. She damn near threw her phone across the room, but instead, she gripped it tightly in her fist. "If anything, he makes me happy so that I'm not stressed! You are the one who is stressing me out right now. I came to you asking for help, Mom, and you keep trying to tell me what to do. It has nothing to do with me. I just want you to help him out."

"From what I heard from your sister, this man has anxiety issues. Neha, I don't think it's a very good idea to go ahead and get involved with that."

"And why not? because he is not perfect by your standards. To Sasha's standards? Oh, the horror. Newsflash, mom, despite his anxiety, he is the one who stepped up and helped me out on the train when I went down. So instead of ridiculing him for something he can't control, you should be thanking him."

There was a long silence on the line.

Neha hung up the phone and set it down on the counter before Sasha walked in.

"Hello, I picked up some groceries." Sasha stopped in the doorway of the kitchen with several grocery bags in hand.

"Why are you looking at me like that?"

"What did you tell Mom about Jane?"

Sasha walked by her and set the bags of groceries on the table. As she began to pull things out, she avoided eye contact with Neha.

"Sasha!"

"What? I only told her about you and him seeing each other."

"Why did you mention his anxiety?"

"I only mentioned it because I was concerned."

"Concerned about what?"

"Concerned that the man might be mentally ill, I don't know, Neha."

"Mental? Because he becomes nervous-"

"Well, we don't even know him that well, Neha. You might like to think that you do, but you don't. You don't know if he's going to end up snapping and doing something horrible to you."

"Unbelievable." Neha shook her head. "Here just a little while ago you were saying he was a hero because he helped me, but as soon as you discover that he has something, he is a demon of some sort."

"I didn't say that, Neha."

"You might as well have. I can't believe you and Mom are blowing this out of proportion. He helped me on the train, and now that he needs my help, I shouldn't be around him. "

"You can't help anyone else until you help yourself."

Neha's face darkened. "Help myself? You are kidding me, right?"

She brushed past Sasha and went to the living room to grab her coat.

"Neha, where are you going?" Sasha called after her but didn't receive a response before the door slammed, rattling the picture frames on the wall.

Jane wasn't sure what to concentrate on as he scanned over job openings and funeral calls to home. He was going back and forth between windows on his computer when his cell phone went off. He glanced down to see a message from Neha. A small smile pulled at the corners of his mouth before he pushed himself away from the computer. He felt a fluttering sensation in his stomach, as if he had just been asked to prom and hadn't read the text yet. He picked up his phone and slipped it open to read Neha's text.

"Are you busy?" it read.

"Not really," he answered.

"Do you want to grab some coffee? My treat. "

29

Life's Simple Pleasured

"Your mom said all those things about me?" Jane asked with a frown as Neha confessed what was wrong. They had travelled to a small coffee shop, and while they waited for their drinks to arrive, he had allowed her to tell him everything that was bothering her. Before she showed up, he had tried to convince her to allow him to come to her, but she was already on her way out when she texted him earlier.

"Please don't take what she said to heart," Neha said, shaking her head. "My mother is just like that, bothered about me always."

"Sasha doesn't know me either."

"That's my family," Neha sighed. "I'm really sorry. I shouldn't have told you what she said. It's better off unknown. "

"No, I'm okay, you don't have to be sorry. It's a nice head's up if I should ever meet her."

"Don't get me wrong, I love my mother, I really do and I love my sister, but they can be such a pain. Ever since I was diagnosed with epilepsy, I feel like they've looked at me differently. I feel like I have to be some bubble-wrapped child of some sort for the rest of my life. They just don't get that I don't have to be monitered all the time, that I can move around freely. "

"No offence, but they do sound like a couple of pains."

"No offence taken, trust me. My dad didn't treat me like that ever. He treated me like I was a normal kid, as if nothing changed after my diagnosis, and I appreciated that the most. "

"I guess on the bright side of the matter, at least you know they care and that's a good thing," Jane replied. "They worry about the people you're around to make sure that you're safe. I think a lot of people in the world wish they had a support team like that behind them. It would probably save them from getting into a lot of trouble. "

Neha turned her head to see him staring at his hands. She reached out and grabbed one of them before holding it in her lap.

She said, "Seems we have experienced both sides of the extreme." "I'm sorry, I must sound like a whiny brat to you."

"No, not at all. I can understand the frustration of having things like that happen." he smiled. "I would never see you as a whiny brat."

"Thank you. But I guess this means that we're back to square one with all the plans that have to be made since my mother won't be of any help."

"Neha, really, you don't have to help me with any of this. It's my responsibility and I will handle it. "

"A funeral should not be placed on the shoulders of one person, Jane. There's so much to it, even if it's a simple cremation. There are the legalities of everything your mother had and such. Where did she go after she left you and your ...him?

"Last I heard she moved to the north."

"So all of her belongings are in the north and her body is being sent here."

"I don't know. I don't know the first step to even going about this. My father had been absolutely no help. I've swallowed my pride and tried to call him, but I guess I've been asked to have my number ignored at the office."

"Your father..." She shook her head. "He's not a father; he doesn't even deserve the title. He's a... Sorry, wait, I probably shouldn't-"

"No," he laughed, "you're right. The biggest and stinkiest of them all. "

He enjoyed the warmth of her hands as she continued to hold onto it. He squeezed it back as she leaned into his shoulder. The two of them offered a smile to the waitress as she brought over their coffee drinks and didn't speak again. The woman had gone to offer some privacy to the topic.

Jane used his free hand to take a sip of his drink but it was too hot before he nearly burned off his upper lip, he decided to wait setting it back down carefully.

"I don't know where to begin with any of this, do you have a large rug that I can sweep it under for the time being?" He asked her.

"Well, unfortunately, I don't have a large rug, but perhaps the first step would be to go discuss all this with a lawyer and go from there. Because the face of the matter is... they won't hold your mother's body forever, Jane.

Eventually, they'll just take it upon themselves to cremate her body and see if anyone will come and collect the remains. Goodness, that sounds horribly morbid."

"Maybe that's what should happen," Jane said, with a slight bitterness to his voice. "Just let them do whatever to her body and have someone else go and collect her remains. I'm not sure if I want an urn with her ashes over my fireplace. "

"You still might be contacted in regards to her belongings and if she had any property, they might call you to discuss the estate."

"I don't want anything from her!" Jane said a bit louder.

Neha quickly shut her mouth and glanced around nervously to see a few people that were in the coffee shop looking over in their direction with concerned faces. She offered a polite smile before she felt Jane's hand shaking in hers.

"I'm sorry!" he exclaimed abruptly, "I didn't mean to get like that!"It's unfair to you. All this anger is directed at my mother. I shouldn't have-"

"Jane, please, you don't have to be sorry. I swear you and I spend half the time we talk apologising to each other. "

"That's a bad thing."

"Not necessarily," she grinned. "It could just mean that we just really care what the other one thinks."

"I think that idea is much better."

"If I am being honest, it's a first," Neha told him. "I normally never care what someone thinks. That sounds pretty bad too. I mean, "

"I understood what you meant," he interjected, leaning back in his seat and looking over at her. A question popped into his head that he just felt the need to ask her. "Why can't life even be this simple?"

"What do you mean?"

"Why can't life be as simple as having a pleasant conversation with a person like you?"

Neha blushed before leaning back and mirroring his actions. "It can be. All you have to do is ignore the outside world."

"The outside world is a very loud place."

"That it is."

30

Too quick to Judge

"So you're just going to not talk to me? At all? " Sasha questioned Neha as she returned that evening from her coffee date with Jane. The girl walked in but didn't look over in her sister's direction, completely ignoring her.

"Do you know how worried sick I've been? You didn't bother to answer any of my calls or texts. I naturally assume the worst every time. Neha, you can't just do that to me. "

Neha continued to childishly give her sister the cold shoulder as well as the silent treatment before she left for her room and closed the door.

"We only care, you know?" Sasha stomped over to the bedroom door, trying to turn the knob, but Neha had been quick to lock it. "We're looking out for you, to make sure that you don't end up hurt. Do you want to end up dying? "

The door swung open seconds later to reveal a very angry Neha, who glared directly at Sasha. Her nostrils were flared and her eyes narrowed, looking about ready to punch her sister in the face for uttering such things. "How dare you even throw that at me!" she hissed.

"But it's true! If you don't take care of yourself, "

"I am taking care of myself!" Neha spat. "I am. I have followed the stupid diet, I've taken multiple medicines, I've discussed surgery... what more do you and your mother want for me? Do you want me to just live in a bubble for the rest of my life? Because I won't have epilepsy, but it doesn't stop me from living my life. It's you and Mom that stop me from trying to live. "

"I—"

"Sure, the seizures could one day lead to my death, but you know what Sasha, so can a million other things, and if all I do is spend time worrying about every little potential thing that could go wrong, I might as well call it quits now. I'm so tired of you and mom trying to control everything I do with the idea that you're doing what's best for me. Because you're not. Neither one of you is doing what's best for me. I want to live my life how I want to, and regardless of whether you two think it's reckless, it's not up to you. It's up to me. I'm an adult now, if you've forgotten. I'm going to make my own decisions. "

The silence fell over the two as they stood on opposite sides of the door looking at each other.

"You really like him, don't you?" Sasha sighed finally. "I've never seen you voice your freedom so loudly until you met him."

"Maybe it's because he listens to what I have to say. He waits until I'm done to voice his opinion and if I disagree, so be it. He doesn't fight me on every decision I make. So yeah, I do really like him. And you and mom would too, if you gave him a chance. But no, you two are so hung up. "

Neha tried to keep a serious look on her face as her sister had failed to miss the point completely, but it was too late for her as she fell into a fit of laughter. "That wasn't my point!"

"I know, but I don't like seeing you all angry and such," her sister said in a soft voice. "It's a bit frightening, to be honest. You get this crazy look in your eye and you make people wonder if that's the last look they're going to witness before they end up dead. "

A small smile replaced the look on Neha's face before she walked over and fell back onto her bed. She stared up at the ceiling after placing her arms behind her head for support, not bothering to grab one of her own pillows.

"Look, you have to understand that Mom and I always worry about you and anyone that you come across. Whether you have epilepsy or not. I'm your big sister and I'll be protective when I damn well please. " Sasha said, crossing the room and sitting down on the bed next to her little sister.

"Jane only makes me nervous because I'm afraid of his anxiety problems that he won't be able to help you one day when you need it. What if he suffers a panic attack while you're on the floor? "

"It's rare that I—"

"I know, the big ones are rare, Neha. I know that. I've been around you long enough, but it doesn't mean that they won't happen."

"I think he handled himself rather well that time on the train. He could have let anyone else handle the situation, but instead he took action. He's trying to fight the anxiety, Sasha, and thinking about all the times he may fail when you should be thinking about all the times he will succeed. He's a strong man at heart; he's just been hurt so many times and it has taken its toll on him. Then to have you and your mother doubt him before properly meeting him, that's not exactly a confidence booster. "

"I'll admit it, I was quick to judge. If anything, if you are talking so highly about him, I want to meet him properly. "

"You do?" Neha sat up and gave her sister a questioning look. She was suspicious of Sasha's intention since the woman suddenly seemed to have a change of heart. She had gone from badmouthing him to wanting to properly meet him. It made Neha nervous. The last thing she wanted was to invite Jane over and have her sister just ridicule him on the spot.

Sasha could be nice, but she did have a mean streak against people that she had already made her mind up about.

"Yes, I do. I want to give him a proper first chance to impress me."

"Sasha!"

Neha's fears seemed to be coming to light as Sasha's intentions didn't sound the best. Jane didn't have to impress anyone, and he certainly didn't have to do it over dinner.

"I'm joking. I want to invite him over and have a nice dinner. Does that sound okay? "

"I suppose so. You're going to make him feel awkward, are you?"

"No, I promise. I'll be on my best behaviour. "

"You said that last year before we went to the Christmas party at Dawn's."

"Yeah well... keep the wine away and we'll be fine."

"You know, you would get along very well with Jane's roommate. Maybe a little too well. I should talk to Jane about getting you two setup so you can stop butting into our business. "

With the plan of inviting them over for dinner, Sasha left the room, leaving Neha with the task of texting Jane and seeing what day would work for him. She wondered if he even wanted to engage in a dinner with her sister. If he said no, she honestly couldn't blame him. Sasha and their mother had not given Jane a chance, being so eager and quick to judge people based on their flaws. Yet, either one of them couldn't stand it if someone did it to them.

31

Over Thinking can be Hazardous

When Mourya got off his last shift, he had every intention of sprawling out on the sofa and taking a much-needed nap after a long day with bitchy customers and lousy tips, but instead walked in to find Jane pacing back and forth. The man was pulling at his hair and had a panicked expression on his face. He let out a heavy sigh, knowing damn well the nap wasn't going to happen anytime soon.

"FCK me," he muttered under his breath. "Jane, what are you doing?"

Jane gave no answer as he dropped his hands from his hair and then began rubbing his palms against his pants. Judging by how his hair was sticking up all over the place, he had been pulling at it hard for quite some time. But usually, during one of his anxiety attacks, he had to do something with his hands or he would start picking at himself. When they were younger, just kids in middle school, Jane had ended up nearly digging a hole into his arms without realising it, getting blood everywhere in his bedroom.

He had learned some coping mechanisms since then, but there were times where he just couldn't bring himself to focus long enough to stop his own hands from causing harm.

"Jane!" Mourya called to him louder when his roommate didn't respond the second time. The man turned his face, his face full of worry.

"Why is it that you always look so terribly concerned?" "What is going on?" Mourya asked him as he set his things down. "What's wrong, dude? Why do you look like someone is about to come kill you?"

"Neha invited me to dinner at her place."

To someone with a normal state of mind, it didn't sound like a problem at all. To Jane, it was the end of the world, apparently. Why? Mourya had no idea, but he was sure he was going to find out within the next few minutes.

"What? Jane, that's great! It sounds intimate and-"

"It's with her sister too, Mourya."

"Hmmmph, I wouldn't have taken Neha to be into that."

"Will you be serious for just a minute, Mourya?" Jane snapped at him. "Just one minute!"

Mourya rubbed the underside of his chin. "I was only trying to lighten the mood, Jane. You're freaking out again, for no reason."

"It is for a good reason. Her sister doesn't like me."

"How could you possibly know that? You've hardly met the woman. She doesn't know a thing about you without actually meeting you."

"Because of the things that she's said to Neha in concern for her hanging around me. She doesn't think I'm good enough for Neha."

"That cow taint, she has no right to pass judgement!" Mourya said hotly. "Who does she think she is?"

"She's Neha's elder sister, who, I'm sure, is just looking out for the well being of Neha, but... I don't know. I don't think I'm going to go. I'll just pretend to be sick or something."

"What? Jane, you're not back in school about to take an exam. She's invited you over for dinner. "

"Right, and you do see the state I'm in right now?! Do you think it's going to look good on my behalf if I show up looking like a nervous wreck? I've been like this for the last two hours. No, it'll just make her sister believe that she was right from the beginning. "

"Ugh, seriously, Jane, you're over-thinking this and it's leading you to get all worked up. Again. "

"I can't help it."

"Yes you can. Right now, instead of pacing back and forth, which is making me incredibly dizzy, by the way, you need to sit down and breathe. Remember, big deep breaths and let it out slowly."

"I don't want to-"

"Too bad."

Mourya stomped over to Jane and roughly pushed the man back onto the sofa. "Now sit there and breathe, dammit."

Jane sat there looking at him.

"Come on, I want to hear it. So there you have it.Good job. Now keep doing that until I change out of these God forsaken clothes. If I don't hear you breathing from my room, I'm going to come back out here and kick you. Even if I am naked. "

The look on Jane's face reiterated that he did not want that to happen at all.

Leaning back on the sofa, he closed his eyes and began inhaling and exhaling as his hands gripped the side of his pants. Using his thumb and index finger, he allowed his fingertips to run over the sofa material, directing his mind to focus on the texture rather than anything else. A few minutes later, Mourya returned and sat on the coffee table across from him.

"How are you doing?" He asked him "Feeling a little better?"

"Yes, a little." Jane nodded.

"Good. Jane, you really need to stop putting yourself down because of what other people say. If I went into a breakdown every time someone insulted him or said something negative about me, I would have locked up a long time ago. People are going to say harsh things, and they are going to pass judgement without getting to know you. It happens. It's human nature. You can't say you've never looked at another human being and judged them without knowing them. If you did, it's a lie. It's just how we work as a species. "

"The problem is, this is Neha's family we're talking about. If I screw this up in front of them, they are going to talk to her about it. What if they convince her not to talk to me again?"

"I doubt they could convince her to do something she didn't want to. She really likes you, man. If she didn't, she wouldn't be spending all this time with you recently. And before you even try, don't you dare say it's out of pity. It's not. It's because she likes you as a person. You accept her with her flaws and all, and she accepts you with your flaws. That's a relationship, Jane. If her family doesn't approve, who the hell cares? It takes time for them."

"I do. I care. I don't want Neha to be upset if her family doesn't like me. I don't want to put her thoughts under stress."

"Dude, you've told me countless times, that Neha is a tough girl, and I can see that. I think she can handle a lot more stress than people credit her for. And if not, you two can be giant stress balls together. Rolling about in a stress factory."

"Gee, thanks, Mourya."

"Anytime." Mourya smiled. "But in all seriousness, Jane, if her sister gives you a tough time, remember that you aren't there for her, you're there for Neha, and she's there for you. And if she really gives you a hard time, call me and I'll come kick her. "

"Right. Okay, I can do this. " Jane said, standing up. "I can put up with whatever her sister has to say to me or about me. Because her opinion doesn't matter to me as long as Neha thinks I'm good enough. "

"Right! That's the spirit. Go get 'em, Tiger."

"Yeah, I'm..." Jane frowned as he sat back down.

Mourya crossed his eyes in frustration. "Stop thinking Jane, just go get dressed."

Jane shook his head.

"What's wrong now?"

"I shouldn't go."

"Why not?"

"Because I have a lot to do right now, I have to contact people about my mother and see what I'm supposed to do. I've been putting it off long enough. I can't put it off for a date. "

"Yes, you can. I'll take care of all that while you're not."

"What?"

"I'm serious," Mourya said, pulling him to his feet. "I will get all that stuff straightened out, but you need to go. You can't keep hiding in this flat behind all the excuses. "

"It's not an excuse-"

"It is, now march to your room, Mister, and put on something tasteful."

"But-"

"Now!"

Jane gave Mourya a bizarre look as he left for his room. However, he returned a few seconds later.

"Mourya, you can't do that stuff without me. You're not in or-"

"They don't know that. I'll just say I'm you. Trust me, I've answered you many times. "

"You have? Why-"

"Don't worry about it. Go get dressed."

32

Neha for Sale

Neha's stomach growled as she sat at the kitchen table reading some news on her laptop. She was skipping over to the weather while her stomach noises continued to grow louder and louder to the point where they were echoing in the kitchen. She continued to try to ignore it, and Sasha seemed to be doing the same until it became too much.

"You ought to eat something; dinner won't be ready in a while," Sasha told her. "But the cops are called because our neighbours think we're harbouring a hungry beast here."

"There's really nothing in the house to eat. I hate all the food we have. " Neha grumbled as she set her chin down on the table and stared up at her sister.

"But you need to eat, Neha." Not eating is just as bad as not following the diet. "

"This diet isn't for me, Sasha. It might have worked in the beginning, but it's just driving me absolutely mental now. All the restrictions... I don't want to do this anymore. "

"You need to set up that doctor's appointment and take them to them," Sasha reminded her. "It's not going to do you any good just to complain about it."

"But they think it's working for me. There's been a reduction in seizures."

"Well, if it's making you miserable, then there should be something they can adjust for you."

"It's a strict diet, Sasha, you know that."

"There are people in the world starving right now, Neha. You should be grateful for the food you're allowed to eat." Sasha scolded her.

Neha hated it when Sasha said things like that to her. She was very well aware of people starving throughout the world and in her own country, but it didn't make the diet she had to be on any easier. But Sasha just loved throwing that in her face, as if it strengthened her argument somehow.

Neha's ketogenic diet was introduced to her as a sort of last resort for the woman. Normally, it was introduced to children as it was easier for parents to control their child's diet. However, for Neha, her doctor recommended it later on when she was older, in hopes that they would see a decrease in her seizures. While she did see fewer of them, it didn't help the fact that Neha didn't want to eat the foods the diet required of her.

Neha saw a lot of it.She could grab at the loose skin that was collecting around her body. Not only was she losing weight, but she was losing muscle as well. The medications didn't affect her mood or eating as much as the diet did.

Her doctor liked her on the diet as they saw results in the beginning. Her seizures had almost become non-existent. The nutritionist had set up the entire diet for Neha to follow along with her family. How many carbs she could eat per day and how she would get her caloric intakeIt was exhausting and irritating for Neha.

It started with Neha having to fast for a day during a stay at the hospital, and then the diet was introduced, in hopes of starting the process of ketosis.

Neha's body was allowed to use her fat as the primary energy source instead of carbohydrates. For the first few days, her mind was grouchy and her body was sluggish as it transitioned. The medical staff had been able to help her in the beginning with monitoring her intake, but when she went home, the struggle began.

She wanted to eat the food that her friends and co-workers ate.

She wanted to share the foods that Sasha ate around the apartment.

She wanted to eat everything she couldn't.

"Make sure you make something that you and Jane can enjoy," Neha told Sasha as the woman rummaged through the cupboards for a certain pot.

"I can make one of your recipes."

Neha shook her head. "I don't want to torture the man with what I have to eat. Go on and make something you'll both like. I'll be okay. "

"I still think you should talk to your doctor."

"I'm going to. But I'm sure they'll just recommend that I stay on it like last time. It's not a matter of what I want, it's a matter of what is going to help decrease the seizures."

"But you're losing a lot of weight, Neha. I think that should bring up some concern on their behalf."

"One would think." Neha sighed, rubbing her head. " I think I'm going to go lie down for a bit. I got a wicked headache. "

"Eat something."

"I'm fine. I just need a nap. "

Sahsa frowned as Neha left for her room. "And yet I wonder why your mother and I worry about you," she muttered.

Sasha allowed Neha to sleep for a good while as she prepared the dinner of spaghetti and meatballs to keep it simple. She pulled some of Neha's leftovers out of the refrigerator for Neha to choose later on. She had some mashed cauliflower with some chicken. Neha remembered that they had always been picky eaters unless it was junk food. So Sasha could only imagine what was going through her younger sister's mind whenever she had to force herself to eat something other than the regular pizza and sweets.

Over time, they had joined websites and followed blogs to find recipes that the nutritionist approved of, but Neha could only eat a meal so many times before she grew tired of it.

Once a while, Neha was allowed to have a small cheat day, but she wouldn't allow herself to indulge, knowing that they would have to return to a strict diet the following day.

"What am I going to do with you, Neha?" Sasha asked, stirring the pot of noodles.

"I suppose you could always wrap me in a blanket and leave me on someone's doorstep." Neha's voice rang out, startling her. "Or put me in a box and put a sign before it saying 'Free'. I am not sure you would get a good amount of money for me."

Sasha laughed. "As if I would ever consider selling you."

"You did that one time when we were kids," Neha reminded her as she sat down.

"We were young."

"You were sixteen and well aware of what you wanted to do."

"I didn't say I was the smartest."

"But apparently you were the most twisted."

Sasha rolled her eyes before pointing to the containers of food. "Is that going to be enough for you or do you want something else?"

"That'll work."

"Are you sure? I can make something else if you want."

"No, seriously, I'm good with that."

"You need to eat more."

The doorbell went off, saving Neha from the lecture going any further.

"I'll get it!"

33

Mr. Maya and Flowers

Jane stood patiently outside of the apartment door as he heard Neha's voice call from inside that she was on her way. He could hear the sound of her feet on the hardwood floor as she approached, and immediately, he could feel his heart rate accelerate as if he had run all the way to her apartment without taking a breather. The minute she opened the door, though, a pleasant warmth filled his body as she greeted him with a smile.

"Hi, Jane!" Neha always looked beautiful, no matter what time of day he saw her, and each time he did, it was the most refreshing feeling to see her smile. It left him weak in the knees and short of breath, but at the same time, it was the best feeling in the world.

He tried to keep a casual tone in his voice, although he was feeling nervous and excited at the same time. "I uh... brought these... flowers!" he yelled as he shoved a small bouquet of colourful assorted flowers in her face, nearly knocking her out."For you!"

She chuckled before taking them gently from his hand. She gave them a small smile before looking up to thank him."Thank you, they're beautiful."

"I didn't know what kind of flowers you liked, so I thought I would go with the variety, although I just realised I never really asked if you were allergic to flowers or had a sensitivity to them. Oh myGod," he rubbed his forehead. "I really didn't think of that at all. I'm so sorry. I can take them back. "

"Jane!" she said, waving her hand in front of his face. A laugh escaped from her, just imagining Jane going back to wherever he had purchased the flowers and attempting to return them while explaining to the vendor that the girl he had bought them for was allergic to flowers. "Hi! Come back to Earth for a second. "

Jane stopped him, holding his breath to refrain from spewing out any more words.

"I love the flowers. No, I'm not allergic to them and no, they won't trigger a seizure, even if they are extremely colorful. They're great. And I thank you for bringing them," she said before leaning in and kissing him on the cheek.

He let a small squeak of delight escape before clapping his hands over his mouth in embarrassment.

"That was also extremely precious," Neha told him. "Now come inside. Sasha has just finished up dinner. "

"I hope she didn't go through too much trouble to prepare the meal." "I'm pretty easy to please when it comes to food," Jane said.

"Don't worry, I didn't go through any trouble," Sasha said, coming into the living room as Neha took Jane's jacket from him.

"Oh, okay then," Jane replied, his nerves setting in quickly.

Neha made a face behind his back, urging her sister to be nicer.

"Oh uh... we never really were properly introduced," Sasha said, stepping forward. "I'm Sasha, Neha's sister."

"I've heard a lot about you, Sasha. I'm Jane Maya. "

"Well, I hope you only heard good things about me, Mr. Maya."

Neha witnessed Jane cringe at being called by his surname and smacked her forehead before glancing at her sister.

"If you don't mind, Jane is just fine with me." Jane informed Sasha as he looked down the hall. "Please."

"Okay, Jane, it is," Sasha said with a slightly irritable tone. She didn't see the big deal with addressing him by his surname, but it was obvious that she hadn't listened to anything that Neha had told her when it came to the relationship between Jane and his father.

"Hey," Neha interrupted, stepping in between the two and smiling at Jane to reassure him that everything was alright. "The dining room is just through that doorway if you want to go make yourself comfortable."

"Are you sure you don't want me to help? I could set the table-"

"No, don't be silly. You're a guest. Go ahead and sit down."

"Alright." Jane gave a small nod and left for the dining room.

As soon as the man was out of sight, Neha quickly reached over and pinched Sasha's arm.

"Ow!" Sasha cried out rubbing,"What was that for?"

"Are you serious? You're making him uncomfortable. "

"Well sorry!" Sasha huffed. "He was being odd."

"You were making him nervous."

"Just by talking?"

"Yes, for goodness sake, Sasha, you're pretty intimidating to a lot of people. You can only imagine how you come across to him right now. At least try to be little nicer, the man brought beautiful flowers. "

"Should I call him Prince Charming then?"

You can call him by what he asked you to call him, which is Jane. You said you would behave. You're an adult, so act like one!" Neha snapped leaving to the dining room.

She saw Jane sitting at the table looking around at everything. A grin appeared on her face before taking the seat beside him.

"I'm sorry about Sasha. Sometimes she comes across a little strong," she whispered to him.

"Oh, no, she was fine. I understand, she's your older sister. She's supposed to be protective, right? "

"Yeah, I guess."

"You guess?" he chuckled. "Well, I don't have any siblings, but I assume it's almost a duty of an older sibling to be protective of the younger one."

"I'm going to get a vase and water for these flowers, and I'll be right back. I'm pretty sure dinner is done. You're good with spaghetti and meatballs."

"Oh no, I'm allergic," he told her with a straight face.

Neha became pale as she stared at him for a moment. "You're aller-"

"Got you," he smiled.

She sighed in relief. "You scared me there for a second."

"Sorry, I couldn't help myself."

"I'll get you back for that." she warned him as she headed towards the kitchen.

"But I was just kidding. Neha? Neha! "

34

Undercooked

After sitting quietly at the table for a few minutes, Sasha walked out and began to serve dinner. While he attempted to ignore it, it was quite obvious that he was being stared down by the elder sister as she kept a watchful eye on him. It was almost as if she was waiting for him to do something foolish or act out, but he wouldn't dream of doing such a thing. He was trying to make a good impression, but he was sure that Sasha had already made up her mind about him without giving him a chance. The tension in the air was thick. Jane wished that if the woman had something to say, she would just say it and rid them of the awkward atmosphere. He looked over at Neha. Normally, she would be the one to woop in to start a conversation to rescue them all, but her focus remained on her plate.

She had hardly eaten anything that was before her, and Jane wondered why she wasn't eating the same pasta dish that her sister had made.

"Neha, would you like some of the bread?" he offered her. Neha glanced up from her plate and gave him a kind smile.

"No, but thank you, Jane," she said.

"Are you sure?" you haven't touched anything on your plate."

"She can't have it!" Sasha replied sharply. Jane dropped the bread basket in a slight panic.

Neha shook her head as she reached out and grabbed Jane's hand that had shakily made its way back to his side.

"I'm sorry, I didn't know."

"It's alright, Jane," she reassured him. "As much as I would like it, I can't have it."

Unlike her sister's barking tone, Neha's voice remained soft and gentle but refrained from becoming condescending to the man.

"Are you allergic to it?" he asked her.

"No, but I have to stay on this diet of low carbohydrates, so pasta and bread are a big no-no as of right now since I've almost hit my mark for the day."

"So when she says no, it means no!" Sasha told him.

"Sasha!" Neha stared at her sister in shock at how the woman was behaving.

"I'm sorry," Jane apologised again.

"You don't have to be sorry, Jane. You didn't know, and it's fine. Sasha is being an utter jerk right now for some reason."

"I'm not being a jerk. I'm trying to show you that he isn't right for you."

Jane didn't walk into the flat with much confidence that evening. However, Sasha had made sure to eliminate any ounce that he had remaining within a matter of seconds. So the dinner had not been for Sasha to get to know him; it was for her to try and point out his flaws to Neha, in the hopes that Neha would try to find someone different. He didn't admit it out loud, but it definitely hurt him to think a person would do such a thing.

"Sasha, stop!" Neha growled, but her sister didn't pay attention to her as Sasha turned to Jane.

"Do you think you can handle my sister?"

"Handle?" Jane repeated, making it sound like Neha was some sort of circus animal.

"Yes, handle her and her condition. You know, she has epilepsy and suffers from seizures, and during those moments she needs someone who is able to take care of her. Not panic. "

Neha couldn't believe her ears. She should have known better that Sasha wasn't going to give Jane a chance. But she didn't know that her sister would go as far as being so nasty to the man as they only tried to enjoy a simple meal. All the nasty behaviour towards Jane over just trying to offer her something to eat. She was embarrassed, but above all, she was furious with her sister's behaviour.

"I am more than capable of taking care of myself," she tried to interject, but Sasha seemed to be out for blood.

"Sure, during the simple seizures you might be able to handle yourself, but what about the one that caused you to drive into a tree or hit your head on the train?! What about those Neha? You can't take care of yourself during those seizures and someone has to be able to. Neha, I don't think that person is you. I'm sorry."

On the verge of tears at how quickly the situation had escalated, Neha removed herself from the table, unfortunately, leaving Jane to face Sasha alone.

Sasha arose to her feet to begin clearing the dishes away, but Jane stopped her as he cleared his throat.

"I'm not sure what your prejudices are against me," he began, "except for the fact that I do have moments where anxiety gets the best of me. Yes, it is a problem. Do you think I don't know that? I'm the one who's had to live with it day after day. I am the one who had to have a functioning career and allow it to not control my life. "

"And where has that gotten you? Last I heard, you're unemployed. "

"Yes, I am unemployed currently, but not for the reason that you think. You see, you don't know me at all and you've already decided to place your judgement on me. I don't have my job anymore because I was tired of working under the tyrant that was and still is my father. The man who holds some of the responsibility for why I don't do well in stressful situations But last time I checked, most people do not handle stressful situations properly. You know what else contributed to me losing my job?

The fact that I was late a couple of times The first time was when I stayed as long as I could at your sister's side when she collapsed on the train. The second time, I was late just trying to work up the nerve to talk with her. But none of that matters to you because you are so preoccupied by my label. That is all you see. "

"That's not true." Sasha went to argue but stopped as Jane looked her straight in the eye.

"Yes, it is, and you know it's true. All you see written across my forehead is anxiety or something along those lines. And when you look at Neha, all you see is an epileptic woman. Neha doesn't want her life to revolve around her seizures, but you do. Everything is about her seizures and not about her. "

"She can't just ignore them."

"And I'm not suggesting she should, but she doesn't have to think about it every second of the day. She has her own life to live. She's an adult and is fully capable of making her own decisions. Am I the best person for Neha? I'm sure, out there, there are plenty of options better than mine. However, right now, Neha has included me in her life, and I will do my best to make her happy for the time that I have. If that doesn't please you, then I don't know what will. Right now, I'm going to go talk to your sister and see if she's okay. Thanks for the dinner. The pasta was undercooked by about twenty minutes, and the sauce was flavorless." "Good night."

35

Pub Love

When Jane walked out of the apartment, he was surprised to see that Neha hadn't gone far from the home, as she was just sitting on the front step. As soon as he stood beside her, she peered up at him with a bright smile.

"I heard you in there," she told him. "What was that?"

"I don't know!" Jane finally let out the breath he had been holding the entire time he had been inside. He suddenly began hyperventilating, realising everything he had said to Neha's sister while he was upset. He could even remember everything he had said, making him wonder if he had said something incredibly offensive to the woman. "But I can't breath!"

Neha's face dropped as she witnessed him enter a state of panic attack. Jumping up at her feet, she quickly reached his side and, while holding onto his arm, she guided him to sit down on the steps with her.

"Breathe, Jane," she said, running her hands up and down his back in a soothing manner. "In and out... slowly."

"Oh God, what did I say?" he asked her.

"What needed to be said? You were amazing!" Neha exclaimed, hitting him on the back by accident. Jane lurched forward a bit, but it seemed to calm him down a bit as a smile appeared on his face.

"I was?"

"Yes, you said what I've been trying to get across for years, and you also stood up for yourself!"

"I did."

She laughed. "Yes! You certainly shut Sasha up. I wish I stayed inside to witness it all. I would have recorded it, just so I could play it over and over whenever she tried to start something with me. "

"No, I'm glad you weren't in there." Jane shook his head. "I shouldn't have done that. I should have been nicer. I was a guest in your home and then... I insulted your sister's cooking. "

"Jane, really, you were in your right to say what you did, even whatever you said about her cooking. She was being nasty and rude. You have nothing to be sorry for and you should regret nothing. "

"I'm sorry for starting this. I should have just listened when you said 'no' to the roll, the first time."

"You didn't know and it's not like I go around announcing it. I probably should have mentioned to you why I was eating something different. I'm sure that did come across as weird. I'll take the blame for that. It was sweet of you to offer the roll, and trust me, I wish I could have eaten it. I'm getting to the point where I'm going to say to hell with this diet and just eat what I want."

"But this diet helps reduce your chances of seizures, doesn't it?"

"It used to in the beginning, but I'm not sure if it's making much of a difference anymore. I do know one thing though... "

"And this is?"

"I really miss real food," she said with a longing look as she started off into the distance. "Like pub food, oh God, I would kill for pub food."

Jane scooted away from her playfully, placing his hands up in surrender just in case there was a slight chance that she might decide to attack him for the sake of food. She giggled before wrapping her arms around his arms, holding onto it and filling Jane's chest with a warm, fuzzy feeling that allowed his nerves to settle and the anxiety to wash away.

"Can you cheat on this diet, just once?" he asked her.

"I don't know. When I mention something like that, the doctors always get their pants in a twist and make me feel bad for even asking. "

"Well, we certainly don't have to tell them," he whispered to her. "It's better to beg forgiveness than ask permission."

Neha raised an eyebrow at him. "I like the way you think."

"It's what Mourya says all the time. Especially on the nights where he's been drinking pretty heavy."

"That sounds like him," Neha mused.

"You know what?" Jane said, clapping his hands on the upper part of his legs. "Let's go."

"Go where?" Neha asked him in confusion as he rose to his feet.

"Somewhere, anywhere. Let's go get you some pub food." He held out his hand to her.

"Yeah?"

"Yeah, Come on! You hardly ate anything during dinner. I won't tell anybody. It'll be our little secret. "

"Alright!" she took his hand, interposing her fingers with his. Jane looked down at their hands as his breath hitched in his throat in surprise. "Lead the way, my good sir," she said.

When they arrived at the pub, Neha was greeted by a few of the gentlemen that were sitting around enjoying a drink.

"I haven't seen you in a while; I just see your sister working all the time," one of the older men said, his pint half-empty.

"Yeah, well I could use a drink myself sometimes," she told him with a wink.

"That's a girl!" Some of the men laughed as Neha pulled Jane along to sit at the counter.

"Do you plan on drinking tonight?" Jane asked her.

"No," she said, shaking her head, "but mentioning drinking gets them all excited.""

Jane looked over his shoulder to see the men becoming rowdy with laughter. "I do," he laughed. "Although they seemed to be quite excited when we walked in."

"Just imagine, they're just getting started."

The two ordered some food and, during their wait, spoke among themselves over Jane, leaving the responsibility of his mother with Mourya. He didn't feel comfortable with the idea that Mourya wasn't going to give him much of a choice.

"Oh Jane, you should have told me," Neha said after a moment where she bit down on her lower lip. "I wouldn't have pressured you into coming if you were taking care of that. It completely slipped my mind."

"No, believe me, I'd rather spend my time with you than worry about that right now."

Neha placed her hand over his hand and gave it a gentle squeeze. He remained still and watched as her eyes studied him for a few moments.

"What is it?" he asked, knowing there was a question itching to be said at the tip of her tongue.

"I'm just curious, I guess, about the world."

"Curious about what?"

"How come you decided to stick with me despite all of my problems?"

"All those problems?" Jane repeated with a confused face. "Besides the seizures, I don't even see that as problematic, just part of you. What else would there be?"

"My family." she reminded him.

"I am in no position to judge anyone and their family relationships. Your family is protective of you. They may not be able to show it properly, but you can tell they care. You don't have all these problems, Neha."

"But the seizures haven't scared you away. I don't know why."

"You're thinking that I'll be like any of your past friends?"

"No, not like them. You're not like them, trust me."

Jane looked away shyly as he finished. His fingers tapped against the wood of the bar as he wondered what her response would be.

"Jane?"

"Yes?"

"Can you look at me? Please? "

He slowly turned his head to face her, only to be drawn into a soft touch.

"S-sorry," Neha began quickly to apologise to him."I don't know what-"

Jane didn't let her finish whatever apology she was going to come up with as he gathered up all his remaining courage and kissed her back.

36

Puddle Jumping

Surprised by his own bold move, Jane pulled away from the kiss after a few blissful seconds, blushing furiously as the men behind them at their table began to bang their hands on the table while hooting and hollering. The loud wolf whistle from one of them caused Neha to turn a bright red as she tucked her hair behind her ear with a smile.

"Seems we have a fan base," she said to him with a light laugh.

"Seems so." Of course, out of all times, his voice decided to crack, bringing him back to his prepubescent years where it happened on a regular basis.

"I, um... wow. I really don't know what to say."

"Is that a good thing?" Neha asked with a hopeful look. It could either be a good thing or a bad thing for someone to be speechless after sharing a kiss although it was a foolish question to ask as Jane didn't look anywhere close to being repulsed by the shared moment. There was also the fact that he had kissed her back, which lessened the chances that it was, indeed, a bad thing.

"Yes, it is a very good thing." Jane confirmed this as he held out his hand to her. Neha watched as it trembled with nerves before she placed her hand over it.

"I really like you a lot, Neha," he told her. "I think I knew since the moment I saw you for the first time on the train. Not in a creepy way, since I didn't really know anything about you. But I guess I just liked the way that you carried yourself and the way you would keep driving yourself day after day, even though some mornings you just looked incredibly miserable. After all this time I've spent with you these past couple of weeks, you've only confirmed it further."

"I really like you too, Jane. I didn't expect all this when I went searching for the person who left me the letter. You really are amazingly sweet and a gentleman. I don't think you understand how rare it is to find these days."

"It... is?"

She nodded. "I think a lot of people have forgotten what a true gentleman is. They are always looking for these bad boys and such, and yet they wonder why they end up so unhappy. It never makes sense to me that they would strive for a man that would treat them so poorly. And unfortunately, it is the gentleman that ends up alone and wondering what he did wrong. "

"That is an excellent way to put it," he said with a nod. "I fully agree. Although I think there are plenty of gentlemen out there who have way more confidence than myself."

"And what does that matter? You're humble, and that's something you don't even see very often anymore. You really should be looking at your pros rather than your cons, Jane."

"It's something I've been trying to do for the longest time, Neha. Believe me, I don't want to think so horribly of myself, but the mind is a very powerful thing. I've been fighting it for so long that it's made me its prisoner. "

"I know," Neha replied quietly. "For the longest time, I found myself with a poisoned mind. I was really bitter about the whole epilepsy thing. I kept asking myself, why me? Throwing myself pity parties for the longest time in the privacy of my room."

37

Take Me Home Tonight

Seated on a bench, the two adults seemed quite content in the company of each other as the night grew later and later. Shortly after the passing storm came to an end, they lost all concept of time. Neha was sure her sister was freaking out back at the house, and Jane wasn't sure what Mourya would make of his tardiness, but neither one seemed to care. As the hour grew later, the streets became even more empty and the two were still damp from running around in the storm and splashing in puddles. She had curled up on Jane's side at once, leaving a bridge of warmth between them, but it was still getting colder.

"This is the best night I've ever had," Jane admitted to her. "Although not the driest, I'll admit."

Neha giggled as she rested her head on his shoulder. "I'm pretty sure if my mother was here she would be all bent out of shape claiming that we would catch a cold for sitting around like this. Then if Sasha saw me, she would be dragging out all the blankets in our apartment to bury me in."

"Well, if you want to, we can head back to your place," Jane suggested. "You should get into something dry. I don't want you to get sick."

She shook her head. "I won't get sick this way, and I really don't want to go back there right now. Sasha is going to have an awful lot to say after all that. I really don't want to be bothered. "

Jane sat there quietly for a moment, trying to figure out how to tell Neha that he was beginning to feel uncomfortable sitting in his damp clothing. There were so many times in his life where situations left him uncomfortable, but he never said anything, in fear that someone would be offended and take his words the wrong way. But the feeling of damp clothing was terrible against his skin, and he wanted nothing more than to just change into dry clothing.

"W-would you like to come back to my place then?" He offered, but he regretted the offer as soon as Neha turned to him, wide-eyed and speechless for a moment. The fear settled in that he had just ruined everything. Neha probably thought that he was coming across too strongly. After all, they had only shared their first kiss. While there were some couples that wasted no time in going back and forth to each other's apartments, Neha didn't seem like that type.

"I didn't mean that in that sense," He attempted to backtrack his words and offer an explanation. "I mean, I want to change the clothing and if you don't want to go home, we have plenty of room at my place, and of goodness, I'm sorry. Please don't take it-I mean wait. I didn't mean that in that sense either. I would like to-No, wait! "

In her whole life, Neha had never met someone who could talk so fast even while nervous. It was like Jane was setting records when he was apologizing, apologising over the silliest of matters and only making it worse on himself as she wasn't even offended to begin with. She had only been caught off guard by the offer.

"Jane," She couldn't help but laugh as she tried to stop the words coming out. "It's fine, I didn't take offence to the offer, it just caught me off guard is all. I wouldn't want you to invite me over just because I'm being childish and don't want to face my sister. If you're uncomfortable in your clothes, then you can go home. You don't have to be polite about it-"

"I wasn't being polite about it. I mean, I was, but I wasn't. That makes no sense." He tapped his forehead in frustration with the palm of his hand.

"Are you saying you want me to come with you?"

"Yes!" He flinched at the over-excitement in his voice, which made him sound incredibly desperate in his head.

Neha pressed her lips together as her legs swung under the bench back and forth.

What would her sister say or think when she didn't return that night? Or what would she say when she found out that she went home with Jane? They had only shared their first kiss and already she was going back to his apartment with him.

Suddenly, she shrugged to herself. She didn't give a damn about what anyone thought anymore as she turned to Jane with a grin.

"Well, what are you waiting for?"

"Y-you want to come back with me..."

She kept her answer short but clear.

"But what about your sister?"

Neha waved her hand to dismiss any thought of Sasha. "I'm a grown up. I'm allowed to make my own decisions and I'm making one right now."

Jane wasn't sure whether to be happy or nervous when Neha agreed to accompany him home. The entire time they traveled, he wondered if they should have stopped by her flat to grab some clothing, but then he figured he would just offer some of his. But which ones? What would she be comfortable in? Should he offer her a bed or sofa?

He was beginning to regret his offer, knowing that he should have thought of everything before he even thought of asking Neha. But it had been a spur of the moment decision; he had seemed to have a lot of little bursts of confidence in the recent weeks of Neha.While he liked it, it also filled him with more worry after the little burst was over because he was left with the consequences of his action. He couldn't even comprehend how Mourya managed to just visit the women's home all the time like it was nothing. Suddenly, Jane's blood ran cold as a particular thought ran through his head.

What was Mourya's reaction going to be?

He groaned silently to himself, knowing all too well how his roommate would respond to seeing Neha enter behind him. Mourya was well known for his adult jokes and innuendos that he liked to make frequently. She would be the first woman that Jane had ever brought to the apartment, and for that, he was certain that Mourya was going to give him absolute hell for it just to mess with him. He figured he had to warn Neha, rather than have her be scared by his crazy friend.

"So, you remember Mourya, right?" Jane attempted to start off the conversation casually, although it didn't sound casual at all. This is just a hurried attempt to get to a specific topic.

Neha glanced over at him. "Of course I do."

"Yeha, right well... You haven't gotten to know him very well given the limited time, but if you're coming back with me, there are some things you should know about him."

"Besides his drinking habits?" she asked curiously.

"It ties in with that," he said. "Mourya is a person that I like to describe as one without a filter."

"Go on."

"As in, he will say whatever he wants and has no regrets. He won't apologise either, especially after a few drinks."

"That's okay," Neha said.

"It is?" he replied, surprised by the calmness of the situation.

"Mmhmm. Does Sasha work as a pub member? I've come across a lot of colourful characters, similar to Mourya. I'll manage. "

"Oh... well... that's good then/But I do apologise beforehand for anything that he says. If you're lucky, he just might be passed out on the sofa already."

38

Knock, Knock

An unpleasant shiver raised down Jane's spine as the couple arrived at the apartment, where he could already hear Mourya yelling some obscenities before they even walked up the steps. Neha liked him. That much Jane was sure of, but would she like Mourya enough to actually have a relationship with Jane? That he wasn't sure of. He couldn't do anything about Mourya either, because the man was the closest thing to family, and Jane wouldn't be able to just get rid of his brother that way. Mourya had been there for one day, helping him with panic attacks and always encouraging him, but he did have the flaws. Some people could deal with them, others couldn't, and Jane wondered what kind of person Neha was.

"Are you sure about this?" Jane asked Neha once more before he thought of opening the door. He was giving her a chance to back out of it, to run, and get away from the apartment as fast as she could. He couldn't blame her if she took the opportunity, especially with the language that Mourya was pewing out. Obviously, his team was not in good standings when it came to whatever scoring.

Neha leaned into his shoulder before she nodded her head. "I'm sure it'll be fine, Jane. Mourya isn't as bad as you think. You're just letting your mind take over with it all."

"You say that, but you haven't known him as long as I have."

After taking a deep breath, he opened the door and allowed her to walk in first. Mourya turned his head from where he sat on the sofa, and immediately the angry face he had from the game he was watching tuned into a smile as he spotted the two.

"Well, hello there," he greeted in an amused tone.

"Hi, Mourya." Neha waved at him, bringing him to wave back in response.

"I should have probably said good evening. "You two are returning awfully late," he said to Jane as Neha looked around the apartment.

"We got caught up in the storm,'" Jane told him, sending a warning glare at his friend.

"I can see that, Neha. You're all wet."

Mourya could see the menacing look in his roommate's eyes, as Jane was probably trying to end his life if he didn't knock it off. Of course, Mourya was amused, but he was actually surprised to see Jane bringing Neha to their home. It was not like Jane to bring people home because normally he psyched himself out, wondering what people would say about the state of the apartment, but it seemed Neha was receiving special treatment.

"I dried off a good amount on the way here," Neha replied innocently.

"Here," Jane said, placing his hands on her shoulders gently, guiding her away from the sofa, "Why don't I show you to my room so you can change into something dry?"

He led her to his room, but while her back was turned, Jane reached out and smacked Mourya upside the head.

Neha looked around Jane's room as she entered. It was everything she expected it to be; neat and clean, very similar to how Jane kept his own appearance. His bed was made and nothing seemed to be out of place. Not even a loose thread on his quilt that was folded over the top.

"Wow."

"Um, is something wrong?" Jane asked her. "Is it the lighting? Is there a smell? An air freshner could be a bit much, but I-"

"No, not at all," Neha cut him off before he got too worked up.Your room is just incredibly neat. I look like a complete slob compared to you."

"Oh well, I highly doubt that. It's just I can be rather clumsy if I keep things out, so I prefer to keep things clean in here to reduce the risk of injury."

"That's... precious."

"Er, yeah. Here, let me get you the clothes. " He quickly made his way over and disappeared into his closet.

Neha could hear him rummaging through things as he mumbled to himself.

He suddenly struck his head out. "Do you have a preference for the material? Do certain fabrics make you itchy? Cotton or Polyster?"

She shook her head politely. "No, I pretty much wear anything. I'm not picky."

"Right." He nodded his head and went back inside the closet.

She waited patiently when he finally returned with a long-sleeved shirt and a pair of pyjama pants.

"I swear I haven't worn either one of these." he said, handing them to her.

"Why not?" she asked.

"The materials... they bug me. I hope they don't bother you."

Neha looked down at the clothing in her hands. It was a simple shirt and the pyjama pants didn't seem out of the ordinary. She glanced back up at him with a curious gaze in her eyes.

"Why do they bother you?"

"It's polyster and it's too rough for my skin. I can really only wear softer materials like cotton. The others just cause skin irritation and... wow, I realised how pathetic that sounded out loud."

"It's not pathetic, Jane. So you have your preferences with clothing, It's understandable. We can only use certain laundry detergents because the perfumed ones ittirate Sasha."

"Thank you," he said. "But you know, I can't let you sleep in those now." He took back the clothes from her abruptly, leaving her slightly dumbfounded as he walked towards the closet again.

"Why not?"

"Because it's going to bother me just thinking you're wearing such rough material."

"Oh no, really Jane, this is-"

There was no reasoning with him as he returned from the closet empty-handed and walked over to his dresser, pulling open the top two drawers.

"I know I have some cotton undershirts in here.... and... I know I have... aha!" He pulled out another pair of pyjama pants. "These will be super comfortable. I promise! I bought these in bulk when they were on sale during festival time because I know they're really soft."

"Thank you again."

"I'll let you change in there. Are you hungry, thirsty, perhaps cold? I have hot chocolate! Would you like to have some hot chocolate? "

She explained that after seeing how excited he was about having hot chocolate, she couldn't say no to a cup.

"Great!" he left the room, leaving her to change.

Neha smiled to herself as she began to strip the wet clothing off, suddenly the door opened causing her to screech as she pressed the clothes to her body.

"Oh my goodness!" Jane clapped his hands over his face. "I'm sorry. I'm terribly sorry! "

His entire face was red, along with his neck and the part of his chest that was exposed.

"I thought... I was going to ask if you wanted marshmellows, but I oh! " He ran out of the room and closed the door behind him.

"Jane's a pervert!" Mourya sang before letting out a laugh.

"Shut up!" Jane cried out as he pulled up his hair. He was already working up a sweat as he began pacing in the living room in front of the television.

"I didn't mean it..."

"Are you sure about that? You've already soaked her-"

"I swear if you make another innuendo, I will break the television and leave you in the darkness."

"Alright!" Mourya gasped as he looked slightly fearful of the threat. "No need to get hostile! I was only joking! "

"What have I done? I should have knocked. Why didn't I knock? Why didn't I knock, Mourya? "

"Oh come on, Jane, you're getting crazed. It's not like you saw anything."

Jane swallowed as Mourya waited for a response. When he didn't say anything, Mourya leaned forward on the sofa.

"Ohhhh Jane! You sly-"

"Quite! I feel horrible as it is. Don't make me feel even more guilty. "

The two men heard the door open, and Neha walked over to them wearing the clothes that hung off her frame.

The three stood in an awkward silence until Neha cleared their throats.

"Can we have that hot chocolate?"

Jane avoided meeting her gaze as they sipped their hot chocolate. To make it worse, Mourya remained close as he continued watching the game. However, ever so often he would turn and smile in their direction.

"I'm not upset," Neha told Jane quickly.

"You're not?"

"No, of course not. I know it was an accident, but it's not a big deal! "

"I should have knocked."

"Knock, knock."

Jane looked up, confused. "What?"

"Knock, knock." she prompted him again.

"Who's there?"

"Dishes."

"Dishes who?"

"You've got a nice place here, Jane," she winked at him. "Thanks for having me over."

"A-a-anytime."

39

Mission Accomplished

'I'm not sure what to do. I've never been in this position before.'

Jane scratched the top of his head as he looked down at the sofa with a look of discontent. His lump of a friend was sound asleep, snoring away with the television still playing in the background. Mourya had drunk himself to sleep, and there was no way they were going to wake him up or get him to move. He had tried in the past, and the results had never worked out in his favor. One time resulted in Jane pulling a muscle in his shoulder, the other with a bloated lip. The initial plan was to give Neha the option of sleeping on the bed that was pulled out of the sofa, but Mourya had made it so that the option was no longer available.

He certainly wasn't going to suggest her sleeping in Mourya's room either; that was a frightening place full of demented dust bunnies, a pink wig, and other random items that would probably scare the living hell out of Neha without trying. Getting into the bedroom would be a task in itself with the cluttered mess, and he wasn't about to put Neha through any of that. But it still left them with the dilemma of where Neha was going to sleep for the night. He scolded himself internally for not coming up with a backup plan of any sort, fully knowing that Mourya enjoyed getting drunk and sleeping on the sofa.

"I can always sleep on the floor," Neha suggested. "All I need is a pillow and a blank-"

"There is no way I'm letting you sleep on the floor," Jane said, shaking his head. "I will not allow that. You're a guest. Just hold on for one second. "

Neha waited patiently as he disappeared back to his room. She looked down at Mourya, whose snoring seemed to grow louder and louder.

"Precious," she muttered as she reached out a finger and poked the man's nose. He didn't even flinch from the touch, making her shake her head in response. "Just precious."

Jane returned and motioned her over to his room.

"I will let you take my bed for the evening, and I can just get my sleeping bag out of the closet-"

"Jane!" Neha laughed. "That's ridiculous. This is your bed. There's no way I'm going to kick you out of your own bed."

"But-"

"We can always share."

Jane's heart skipped a beat as she suggested sharing. Actually, it didn't skip a beat, it exploded in his chest and stopped all blood flow in his body, leaving him in a blank stupor for a few moments.

"I...um.."

"Unless it's weird for you, Jane. But I honestly don't mind sleeping in the bag while you sleep on your bed."

"No!" he said abruptly, but then clapped his hands over his mouth. He felt like Neha was going to think he was a complete lunatic by his antics if she didn't think that already. But judging by the smile that remained on her face, she didn't look very upset with him or disturbed.

"I promise I'll behave," she told him. "I know how to keep my hands to myself."

Neha had no idea how her words affected him, how just the simplest of teasing caused him to work up a sweat and get him feeling half-crazed. She didn't understand that sleeping in the same bed as she would be a dream come true, but Jane lived so long in nightmares that he wasn't sure if he could handle the dream.

"O-kay. Sure, we can do this. I can do this." he said the last part to himself. "Um, you can get in first."

Neha could see the stress on Jane's face as the man laid down on his bed facing her. She had to admit that it was more comfortable. The sheets were softer than anything, everything was comfortable, but that wasn't enough to distract her from the uncomfortable look on Jane's face.

"Jane, if I really make you feel that uncomfortable-"

"No, it's not you. I swear," he said. "It's me. It's always been me."

"Why are you so hard on yourself, Jane?" she asked, already knowing the answer. "I wish you could see yourself the way I see you."

"I wish I could see myself the way you see me too. But it's not that simple—"he stopped talking as her hand reached out and touched the side of his face. At first, he flinched and Neha took it as a clear sigh to move her hand away from him, but instead, as she went to move, he placed his hands over hers. Her hand remained over his cheek, he could feel the warmth.

"You really need to be kinder to yourself," she said softly.

"I'm learning how. everyday You should have seen me when I was younger. If you think I'm bad now, you would have had me institutionalised when I was younger. "

"No, I wouldn't have. I would have had the people who did this to you imprisoned though," Neha said. "That's for sure."

"You mean my father?"

She nodded.

"It would have been nice to have him arrested. But I don't think they would imprison him just for being a horrible parent."

"Well, then we could banish him to a faraway land. Or maybe a volcano somewhere. An active one preferably. "

The smile reappeared on Jane's face as the mental image appeared in his mind.

"That sounds like fun," Jane said, "but just putting him in the middle of nowhere so he can't run his dictatorship of a company would be amazing as well."

Jane's pupils dilated.

"Too much?" she laughed.

"No, that sounds about right."

It didn't take Neha very long to fall asleep beside him. At one point, her eyes were growing heavy and it seemed she was fighting to stay awake, but she was losing the battle. He watched as her eyes closed for the final time and didn't open again. Her breathing slowed down drastically as she slipped into her sleeping state. Her hand had slid down from her face, where it had still rested on her cheek, down to her shoulder and remained there.

While he was incredibly happy to have her beside him, Jane was also a nervous wreck on the inside. He wasn't sure if Neha would suffer from a seizure during the night. What if he didn't hear her? He thought about staying up all night to make sure she would be okay.

But as he fought sleep to stay awake, sleep overpowered him as his eyelids grew heavier and heavier. As much as he wanted to stay up through the night, his body was not allowing it.

Mourya sat up on the sofa once he heard the flat grow quiet. He stood up and turned the television off. Leaving to check up on the two, Mourya saw the two asleep and chuckled to himself as he walked to his bedroom.

"Worked like a charm. I'm a freakin' genius."

40

Morning Breath, Pride and Prejudice

As much as he wanted to enjoy the luxury of sleeping in, Jane was the first person in the flat to wake up the next morning. For some reason, he believed everything that happened the night prior had all been some amazing dream his brain had concocted while he slept. However, as he opened his eyes that morning, he found Neha still asleep across from him, if only by a few centimeters. Apparently, during the night, the two of them had either gotten cold or felt the need to flutter in their chests. He remembered he had vowed to stay awake to make sure she was okay through the night. Realizing he had failed to keep the silent vow, he began glancing at the woman to make sure she was okay.

Neha continued to sleep peacefully, as Jane observed. Her face was calm and relaxed, her eyelids flickering at the touch of his fingertips tickling her cheeks. Although he didn't realise that he was moving her hair over her face, brushing it against her nose.

"You're tickling me," her startled voice rang out before she let out a light laugh and slowly opened her eyes to adjust to the morning light in the room.

Jane quickly pulled his hand away. "I'm sorry," he apologized. "I just want to make sure that you... you were."

"Alive?"

"That sounds horrible on my behalf, doesn't it?" "I'm really sorry, Neha. I can be such an idiot sometimes."

"Jane." She stopped him with a patient smile, resting her hand on his chest. "It's okay. You think you're the first to check on me after a night of sleep? Trust me, I'm quite used to people checking to see if I'm still breathing in the morning."

Jane's thoughts raced to the idea of Neha's family doing the same as he did, swallowing hard.

"Sasha has done it a lot of times, especially when I was younger, because I was a real heavy sleeper and I wouldn't wake up right away when someone was calling my name. But my father spent a whole night by my side when they first learned of my seizures," she told him. "No matter what the doctor said, he was quite set on making sure."

"Do you have seizures in your sleep?" Jane asked her.

"I do...rarely. But they aren't bad ones if I do. You would hardly be able to notice them. The only way they detected them was through a sleep study when I was younger attached all this stuff to my head... I looked like something out of a horrible sci-fi movie." Neha smiled, "although I did get to eat dinner, which was nice."

"Sorry for interrupting your sleep," he said.

"Don't be. I'm not even sure what time it is, but I felt well rested. Your bed is incredible to sleep on. Comfiest. "

A sense of pride washed over Jane, even though it was really his bed that was receiving praise and not him. "Thank you," he said, "I worked extra hard to get it to this taste. I absolutely hate uncomfortable beds. That's why I don't really stay overnight anywhere but here... if I had to travel for business, I would push myself to get home to sleep. Hotel beds were never something I could get used to."

"I don't blame you, I would do the same for this bed."

Neha sat up and stretched her arms before looking over at him. "You know, I completely neglected the fact that I didn't bring a toothbrush... and here I am probably killing you with my morning breath. I should be the one apologizing. You didn't have to be nice about it; you could have just told me."

"Oh no, I didn't mind-I mean anything. I mean, I don't know what I mean," he sighed as he rubbed his hand over his forehead.

"This is probably going to sound incredibly weird, and I'll apologise in advance, but I have a toothbrush that you can use. It's never been used. I have a lot of them there."

"Really?" Neha raised her brow. "What for? Do you use one a day and then throw it away? I had a friend like that back in high school. I always felt bad, but she couldn't handle the idea of germs, so she would throw a toothbrush out after use each time. Terribly wasteful. I guess she couldn't think of another suitable solution. But enough rambling... you can talk now."

"Well, when you've known Mourya for as long as I have, you get used to his habits," Jane explained."

Neha grinned at the man's awkward shuffle as she scooted to the edge of the bed to look up at him. "You've brought supplies for your rommate's one night stand?"

"Is that bad?"

"NO!" she laughed, shaking her head and waving her hands. "That's the sweetest thing I've ever heard of. You must be a godsend to those friends."

Jane gave Neha a spare toothbrush and showed her all the products he had that she was free to use if she wanted to shower.

He left her to take care of her business while he went to the kitchen. He found Mourya awake, nursing a hangover with a cup of coffee and a cup of water in front of him. He was debating which one he should drink first. When Jane walked out, though, Mourya seemed quite pleased to see him.

"Morning, baby." Mourya smiles at him.

"Don't call me that," Jane replied.

"Oh come on," Mourya said. "I'm only teasing, anyway, you and Neha."

"Nothing of the sort happened. I let her go to sleep and I went to bed myself."

Mourya's expression dropped. "You're kidding me? You are freaking kidding me Jane!"

"What?"

"You think I faked sleeping on the couch so you and Neha could have a slumber party?"

"What did you expect? In order for us to...

"Yes really! After all this time, I figured... ugh, you two killed me. This isn't fckng pride and prejudice. Jane, you don't have to court the girl around for months before getting, Hell, a lot of girls think you're crazy when you just ask them on a date."

Jane's face grew stern. "Well, perhaps I would like instead of just, I really really like her and I don't want to rush anything at the risk of ruining anything."

Mourya sighed. "Fine, fine, Mr. Darcy, go have fun courting Miss Bennet."

"I will!"

41

No Bad Boys, Only Gentlemen Allowed

Neha couldn't pretend that she couldn't hear the discussion that Jane and Mourya were having out in the living room as she finished up in the washroom, trying to freshup herself for the morning. While Jane was trying to keep his voice low, Mourya was not one to whisper, and when the discussion of togetherness came up, she instantly saw her face turn a bright red in the mirror. Obviously, her intentions of coming home with Jane were viewed differently by Mourya, but she didn;t have any intentions of sleeping with Jane right away. Neha was not one of those people that could leap into someone. Although it didn't sound like that since she had kissed him the night before and then.

However, Jane reassured her without realising that he had no intentions of rushing anything in their relationship, and for that, she was incredibly thankful. So many women could claim that they wanted bad boys, but Neha knew damn well that she didn't want that. She wanted a man first, and most importantly, she wanted a gentleman. If Jane wanted to be Mr. Darcy, it was almost too perfect in her mind. She would gladly accept having a Mr. Darcy over someone who was just preoccupied with the idea.

Neha, like many other women who struggled with their image on a daily basis, was extremely self-conscious about herself.

She was underweight, she suffered from seizures, and her family was on the mental side. Neha couldn't figure out what would be so appealing about any of that. While she had those flaws working against her, Neha hoped she could charm Jane in other ways. The more they would learn about each other, they wouldn't focus on their own flaws, but on all the things that the other liked. They wouldn't focus on their own flaws. When Jane told her that she was a beautiful piece of art, she couldn't even stop herself from kissing him.

No man had ever complimented her in such a way. Some believed that flattery just came in the form of saying they had eyes or that they looked good in a dress, but Neha wanted more than that, no matter how selfish it sounded. I was nice to be complimented on something physical, but it wasn't everything. If someone could compliment her on something she struggled with, it drew her mind elsewhere, completely distracting her from her insecurities.

She opened the door slowly and saw Mourya in his room, closing the door behind him. While Jane stood at the end of the hall, patiently waiting for her. She walked out quietly and made her way towards him. Despite what he heard, he turned around. As soon as he saw her, a smile appeared on her face, and it made Neha's heart flutter. The way he smiled at her made her feel more beautiful than any other person in the world, even if she had been looking at her in disgust just a couple minutes prior.

"I heard what you said," she told him, folding her hands in front of her. She watched as Jane ran his hand over his mouth and avoided her gaze.

"You did?" He muttered. "I'm so sorry."

"Don't you dare apologize," she said before letting out a laugh. "You cannot stand here and apologise for being a true gentleman. I won't allow it."

He peered up at her, a hint of a smile on his lips as he met her gaze for a brief moment. "So you heard everything about Mr. Darcy and courting?"

"I did," Neha said, nodding."Now, we don't have to actually go that far back, but I will take you being a gentleman and us taking things slow. I really like you, Jane."

She had confessed it, and while she figured that she would have panicked before getting it out, she felt awfully confident in that moment. She wanted him to know that she really liked him, not just for her sake but for Jane's as well. He lacked self-esteem and too many times she heard him claim that he wasn't good enough. Now he had someone like Sasha telling him the same thing, but she didn't believe that. Not for one second. Jane was good enough. In fact, he was too good. It was unfair that people used his flaws against him instead of looking at how refreshing it was to date someone that didn't boast about themselves and put the other person before them.

"I-I-I really, really like you too, Neha," he admitted in return, although he would not be able to look her in the eye as he said it. There wasn't a problem with it; she actually preferred it. Sometimes, people were too much when it came to eye contact, and she found it intimidating and creepy.

Perhaps it was because Neha believed that she wouldn't be able to find someone who would be willing to put up with her health problems. But that was limiting herself because she wasn't as happy as she could be. She just assumed it was as good as it was going to get. Then she met Jane, and it was as if a veil had been pulled away, revealing a completely different experience.

"I just wanted to thank you for being so sweet and respectful about everything, it's really hard to find that," she said to him. "So thank you."

"You never have to thank me for something like that, Neha. I think it's sad that we live in a world you don't expect this, that you actually feel the need to thank me," Jane shook his head. "It's not right."

"I know, but I wanted to thank you, at least until the world decided to get better."

"Well, you're very welcome," he replied. "Now do you want to go out and get some breakfast and then I can take you home? I wasn't sure if you wanted to call your sister and let her know that you were okay. I'm sure she was worried last night."

Neha shrugged her shoulders. "That's what she gets for being rude, but yes I would love to get some breakfast with you. Where did you have in mind?"

"I don't know, but I'm really in the mood for Idly. What about you?"

"Idly sound great."

42

Brain vs. Brawn

The couple enjoyed their breakfast, which consisted of pancakes and syrup, and neither one of them wanted it to come to an end. They dragged it out for as long as possible, but with Neha's cell phone dead in her pocket, she was sure that Sasha was going to end up sending the special force team to look for her if she hadn't already. Luckily for her, Jane agreed to accompany her home, hoping that he could talk to Sasha and perhaps start over, to make it easier for Neha. If they actually wanted to pursue a relationship that would end up being serious, he couldn't expect Neha to deal with him and her family clashing, even if he wasn't doing anything. He was sure that she would choose her family over him, especially since they had been through a lot together with Neha's condition.

He didn't want her to even think about having to make such a decision; that certainly wouldn't be fair to her and he didn't want to put her through such a stressful state. It would not do her any good, especially with her condition.

As they grew closer to her house, Jane could already feel the tension building as Neha pressed his hand. Normally, he would have melted like butter from just the sensation of her holding his hand, but she was holding it because she was nervous. She was probably expecting the same kind of drama, perhaps even more than what Jane was anticipating. She did know her sister a lot better and knew what the reaction would be. He decided to hold her hand in return to offer some comfort silently and to also soothe his own nerves.

"Do you think she's going to be really upset?" Jane asked her. "I really think we should have called her last night."

"She was going to be upset even if I did call her last night, Jane. She'll find a reason to be upset about anything. Don't let her intimidate you or get into your head. It's what she liked to do, Sasha's always been the type that will try to get into your head and use whatever your weakness is against you. She did it to me for the longest time. She especially loved using guilt to get into my head, and she'll try to do the same for you. Don't worry though, I'll help you and..."

Neha stopped in the middle of the sidewalk as they neared her apartment, her grip loosening on his hand as she started straight ahead.

"Shut," he heard her mumble before he turned to her.

"Neha, what's wrong?"

He followed her gaze, and immediately, his face drained of all colour as he looked in the same direction and saw Sasha standing outside with a man, looking right at them. Judging by what he had heard from Neha about her past, that man was Arjun.

"Oh dear."

As they grew closer to where Sasha and Arjun were standing, Jane felt like he was staring down a rather large gorilla. Arjun wasn't really large in comparison, but he had a brutish look to him; he had wider shoulders, his brow was thicker, and he just looked like he could beat up Jane and down the sidewalk.

"Neha!" Sasha ran over and wrapped her arms around her sister, nearly shoving Jane to the side. The woman glared in his direction, causing Jane to look down like a submissive puppy before Neha attempted to break away.

"Sasha... sasha... sasha, stop!" Neha finally managed to push her away. "Stop it! I'm alright, goodness. "

"Yeah, and how the hell was I supposed to know that?" Sasha looked absolutely livid as she stood a couple of feet away. "How was I supposed to know? Last night, you just disappeared, and I had no idea where you went! You didn't take any of your medication with you! For all I knew, he could have taken you against your will..."

"I swear to God, Sasha, just stop before you make a further fool of yourself!" Neha growled. "The only reason I left last night was due to your behaviour. You were terrible last night, and here you are still trying to blame him. And what is he doing here?"

She pointed over in Arjun's direction as the man walked over, still staring Jane down. Neha was a hundred percent on the verge of just losing her temper and exploding on everyone except Jane. She could see Arjun just eyeing Jane like he was some inferior being. She could see Sasha at him. She could see poor Jane shaking.

"I showed up when your sister called me during the night and told me that you just took off or there was a possible chance that you disappeared with some stranger," Arjun said. "So this is him? This is who?"

Jane's self-esteem has been taking hit after hit since they showed up. They thought he kidnapped Neha against her will, they were looking at him in such a horrible way, and obviously, he did not stand up to Arjun's appearance.

"Alright, that's it!" Neha's confidence was soaring at that moment as she placed Jane behind her. "Let's get a few things straight, shall we? I left last night because my sister suddenly forgot her manners and how to treat a fellow human being. Both of you are being judgemental, but believe me, I've seen both of you at your worst and neither one of you can say anything about anyone else. But if you both need some reminders.. "

She stood between the other two, with Jane peering over her shoulder as Neha pointed at Sasha.

Pushing past the two, Neha pulled Jane behind her and made her way to the door of the apartment.

"Neha, what are you doing?" Sasha stomped her foot. "Where are you going?"

"I'm going upstairs with Jane. I'm going to pack my things and I'm moving out! " Neha told her. "I'm moving out of this apartment and getting away from you. From the two of you actually. "

"What? Are you insane?" Arjun huffed at her, stomping over. "You're being irrational. Are you on new medication or something, Neha? This is stupid. What?

Are you going to move in with him?"

Neha was obviously growing too upset to keep speaking as she looked away and wiped her eyes with the sleeves of her shirt. Jane was so tired of the way they were looking at him and the way they were talking to Neha when she had done nothing wrong.

"Even if she was moving in with me, that's none of your business," Jane said, looking at Arjun in the eye for a brief second before staring down at the ground.

"She's not your friend anymore, and even if she was, you don't have any say over what she does. Neha is her own person and she can do as she pleases, and if that means getting away from people who are bringing stress into her life, then so be it."

"She was doing just fine before you showed up!" Sasha shouted at him. "She was very happy."

They heard Neha scoff loudly, and the three glanced over at her. She shook her head before she looked directly at her sister.

"You honestly think I was happy? Every morning, I'm crying to myself or scolding myself before bed, trying to figure out what's wrong with me and why my life can't be easier and you think I'm happy? Why? Because you were happy because you were in control, automatically I should be happy, right? Well, that's not how it works, Sasha. For the record, I've been pretty fckng miserable. With everyone telling me what to do and how to live, as I'm not a person with my own thoughts, I go to work where I already feel like hell, just to come home and be reminded that I am some sort of burden on your life. But yes, I'm so happy... just so happy! "

Without another word, Neha began climbing up the stairs to the apartment, and not wanting to be left alone with Sasha and Arjun, Jane followed her. He could hear her crying as she continued up. He wanted to say something, but he wasn't sure what he could say. Obviously, he didn't want to say sorry; he had done nothing wrong, but he didn't like seeing her upset. He hated hearing her cry and not being able to stop it right away. He hated the two for making Neha feel that way.

But more importantly, another question ran through his mind: Was Neha planning on moving in with him?

43

Are we moving Too Fast?

As soon as Neha found herself standing in her bedroom with Jane entering close behind her, she closed the door and leaned her back against it. A heavy sigh escaped from her lips, although Jane could sense how shaky she was. Her hands were trembling against the wood of the door, and her eyes closed as she tried to calm herself down. A lot of anger had surged through her body in such a short amount of time, anger that she had been bottling up for quite some time with really no outlet for her to vent. She wasn't the type of person to unload all of her problems on a person, and it seemed to take its toll on her as she continued to just remain so calm on the outside, while she screamed on the inside.

"I don't know what I saw in him," she finally spoke as she opened her ears. But she didn't look at Jane as her eyes focused ahead, staring straight at the wall. "I really don't. Ever since, all I've noticed are all the bad things about him, and it makes me wonder."

From what he had witnessed in the brief encounters with Arjun, he certainly didn't like the way Neha thought about herself after she had seen him. For him to question her medication intake as if it were any of his business and then to insinuate that she was the one in the wrong, left Jane disgusted. He couldn't even get started on Sasha. She had been just as bad, if not worse. To say such things to her sister, knowing that it would upset NEha, was as if they didn't care in the slightest.

He didn't believe that they didn't care, but they certainly didn't know how to show it in the appropriate way. However, the question had yet to leave his mind. Neha had claimed that she was packing her things and moving out, but Jane didn't know if she meant that she was moving in with him.

As beautiful as the idea sounded, Jane wasn't sure if he was ready for such a thing. It might have sounded silly to others, but he and Mourya had a routine in their apartment that they both worked with. Adding a third person to the mix would take some getting used to during an adjustment period. But would Mourya be okay with it? More importantly, would Neha actually like living with them? It was one thing to be an overnight visitor, but living in the same household permanently was a completely different scenario.

"So are you going to pack up your things?" Jane asked her as he sat on the edge of her bed. Neha walked over and sat behind him before shaking her head.

"No," she said quietly, pacing."I'm pretty much all bark and no bite, Jane. Where the hell am I supposed to go? I can't live on my own, even if I wanted to. Even if I tried, my mother would be somewhere having convulsions. If she knew I was moving out, she would try to bring me home, and I can't bring myself to do that either."

"But you're going to be unhappy if you stay here, Neha," Jane frowned. "That's not healthy at all, and that's not fair to yourself. You stuck up for yourself today, and you stuck up for me too. Don't let your words be for nothing."

"Then what do I do?" She said to him simply. "Where do I go? I would rather live in a freaking 'box outside of the train station than stay here, but I can't. I can't be alone, not with how the seizures have been in recent times. Something could go wrong. I know I always get annoyed when others worry about me, but I'll admit, I'm scared about being on my own sometimes too. I don't want people constantly checking over me, but there are times where my thoughts get the best of me and all I can think of is, what if no one is home and something bad really happens? What if someone doesn't get to me in time and... "

She shook her head as her voice trailed off for a moment; her hand rubbed over her forehead, back and forth as she tried to self-soothe.

"My mother and sister don't want me to end up like that, and I don't want that either."

Jane slowly but steadily reached his hand out and removed her hand from rubbing a sore spot in her forehead. He placed it down in his lap, where he held it gently for a few moments. It remained quiet as he tried to figure out the appropriate way of wording what he wanted to say to her.

"I understand the fear of being alone and on your own, Neha. Believe me. It may not be for something such as epilepsy, but I have never been on my own either because I've had my own fears about it. It's why I've lived with Mourya for so long and he's been wanting to go out on his own for a while too. But he's a good person. He's out of his god damn mind most days, but he's always been amazing,"

Neha smiled at him before she gave his hand a gentle squeeze. "I'm really glad that you have someone like him in your life. After what you've been through with your parents, I think that it's beautiful that you were given a brother, even if he's not blood."

"Yes and I'm incredibly thankful for him, every single day. But I guess what I was getting at is, I could be that person for you as well if you'd like?"

Jane could feel his throat tighten and it was suddenly becoming hard to breathe and swallow. He was offering her to move in with him despite having only a handful of dates with her and only sharing a first kiss.It was beyond a bold move; it was ridiculous. He wasn't sure what he had been thinking or if he had been thinking at all. He had thrown logic to the wind ever since he met Neha; everything he had been so afraid of doing before, he was just going with the flow. He was certain he was going insane with what he was doing. had come over him and his mind.

Asking a girl to move in with him? The same girl that he couldn't even approach on the train for months.

"Are you suggesting that I move in with you?" If Neha's voice grew any quieter, Jane was going to have to acquire some hearing aids because he could barely hear the girl.

"Y... yes."

44

Mourya's special

There was no attempt at lying when Neha claimed that she was all bark and no bite. She normally could say things, but going through with them was an entirely different thing. She had voiced for months that she was going to go to her doctor and tell him to take her off the stupid diet, but that never occurred because as soon as she got to the doctor's office, she only found herself nodding her head. The doctor would recommend medications, tell her what she needed to do, and then see her off with a new prescription while Neha never got to voice what was on her mind. As soon as she left the doctor's office, she became angry with herself for being so weak.

Outside, she had put Arjun and Sasha in their place before claiming that she was moving out, but Jane had brought up a very valid point, that she couldn't just say things and not act. There he was, being the knight in shining armor, offering her to move in with him. She wanted to blurt out a yes, knowing very well that he would be a gentleman to her as he normally was, but it still felt like it was moving so fast.

There were couples that spent time together intimately on meeting; there were people married within a month of meeting; but Neha wasn't one of those people. For so long, everything had to be planned out, and even then she needed a backup plan afterward. It was a scheduled life a lot of the time, with medications and doctor's appointments early on. Her sister's schedule had been moulded around hers to make sure that Neha was never truly alone, and when Sasha had to work, the neighbour was there to check in on her.

"I don't know Jane," she said with a heavy sigh. She wished she was the type of person that could easily agree to anything without worrying about the consequences, but it just wasn't the type of person she was. She had to think of every consequence of her actions because it was possible for them to be life-threatening.

"I understand, Neha," Jane said quietly. "It was a really forward suggestion, and I was foolish to suggest such a thing. I just didn't want you to feel trapped here. I know that feeling of not being able to more freely. I didn't want you to feel that. You don't have to live with me, but I think we can find an apartment that will accomodate your needs. Just so you're not putting yourself in danger."

Everything in life poses a danger. If Neha was being honest with herself, there was a possibility of walking out of her apartment one day and being hit by a swerving truck. It was unlikely, but it could happen. So, if she spent the rest of her life worrying about all the bad things that could happen, she would miss out on a lot of good.

"Wait," she said, "Can we do it on a trial basis?"

Her question seemed to confuse Jane, as his eyebrows knitted together for a moment. "I'm afraid I don't follow."

"I'm not ready to make a full leap, Jane. You know, I only moved all my things back here a short while ago. But maybe this all could work out. I'd live with you... and Mourya. So maybe, instead of moving all of my stuff out, I can just move some of it in. Some of my clothes and things I'll need, just to see how it would work. If it does, then gradually I can move my stuff and if it doesn't, then it won't be as bad."

Jane was fully aware that Neha was trying to be realistic, but it still wasn't working out. The only way it wouldn't work out was if she grew tired of him and his anxiety or if she didn't want to live with Mourya around. He could never think of sending her out, even if he had to witness seizures. But he knew that she didn't say things to hurt his feelings, she just had to make sure to watch out for herself.

"That... that sounds fine. If that's what you want," he told her. "Just because I offered it, doesn't mean you should feel obliged, Neha. It's up to you."

Neha hopped up to her feet with a bright grin and made her way over to the closet, pulling out a duffle bag.

"So, are you going to help me pack a couple of my things?"

Sasha and Arjun attempted to put up the biggest fight and argument to prevent Neha from leaving. Sasha even threatened to call their mother to stop Neha, but the girl reminded them that she was an adult and even if her mother and family didn't agree with it, there was nothing they could do. She was free to make her own decisions as she pleased. The only thing that epilepsy prevented her from doing was driving away, which she would have loved to do while honking the horn obnoxiously loud as she departed down the street.

Arjun continued to blame it on her medication, claiming that it affected her mind and caused her to make poor decisions. He recommended that Sasha call Neha's doctor, which was the final straw for the woman as she threw her bag over her shoulder and grabbed Jane's hand, leading him out of the apartment.

"Can you believe those two? The nerve they have! That's always been the way to one... up during an argument. They always blame my medicine! Whenever I don't agree with them to follow orders like a damn, they think I need a change in my medicine. Idiots, both of them. They are perfect for each other: obsessive, controlling, and stupid. I hope they get together."

Jane listened quietly as Neha ranted. He really wished that she didn't allow the two to get her worked up, as she was fearful it would trigger a seizure with the amount of stress she was carrying. He knew there would probably come a time where he witnessed one of her bad seizures, not just finding her lying on the ground or a small one in the library. But he didn't want that day to be right then. He grabbed both of her hands without saying a word and held them in his lap.

Neha seemed to pick up on the hint and quieted down before leaning her head back and closing her eyes to relax for the rest of the train ride.

Mourya heard the voices of Jane and Neha coming up the stairs, initially bringing a smile to his face, so proud of Jane for bringing back the girl for the second time. The man was deviating significantly from his norm.However, he heard Neha's voice, and she didn't sound very happy. Jane walked into the apartment first, carrying a duffle bag, while Neha remained outside the door on the phone.

"What's going on..." Mourya looked over the couch as Jane set the bag down on a chair.

"She's on the phone with her mother, who called her thirty-two times on the train until Neha picked up. Apparently, she's very adamant about Neha not moving in here."

Mourya nearly fell off the couch as he stared at Jane in bewilderment. "She's moving in? Jane, what the fu.. "

"Look, I will explain it all clearly! But right now... right now. " Jane began pulling at his hair, pacing the floor.

The other man looked back and forth between the two adults before picking himself up and going out to the kitchen and coming back with a small paper plate full of brownies. He held it out to Jane first.

"Wh..what are you doing?"

"Just eat it, Jane; it'll make you feel better. Trust me, chocolate makes everything better."

Jane eyed Mourya suspiciously before taking one and biting into it before Mourya went over and offered one to Neha. She seemed confused like Jane, but took one before yelling back at her mother. Mourya went back and forth between the two, allowing them to continue and waiting for the effects to kick in.

A little while later, Jane sat down on the couch beside him and placed his legs up on the coffee table.

"How are you feeling?" Mourya asked him.

"I feel... I feel... really nice." Jane smiled.

"Good," Mourya said, "Because those brownies weren't freakin' cheap."

"What was in those brownies anyway?" Jane asked as Neha came in quietly and sat down, appearing relaxed as well. Mourya looked at the two before smiling.

"Love. Just call it Love."

45

The Morning After Chill

Mourya realised that he probably should have monitored the two closely with how many brownies they ingested as they were special "edibles" that were not made to be consumed in large amounts in such a small time frame. He usually got one or two to do the trick for him during the evenings, but he had also built up his tolerance over the years. Jane's and Neha's systems were clean, practically pure as they never drank or participated in other activities, leaving them highly vulnerable to the effects of the drug, especially since they were a stronger dose of cannabis-infused food. They weren't given a chance to gradually build a tolerance and the effects were a lot faster as they became as active as couch cusion later on in the night.

They were relaxed, which was nice to see as Mourya hated seeing Jane worked up and he certainly didn't like seeing Neha in distress. The other two adults just sat around for the rest of the evening, eventually. Neha came to sit by Jane's side, and the two curled into each other, preparing to fall asleep. Mourya knew what was going to happen in the morning. He had already seen the suspicious look on Jane's face earlier when he had first offered the brownie, but Jane was in such an upset that he had looked past Mourya's lying and went for it. He knew that Jane was going to be extremely upset, and he wasn't even sure what Neha's reaction was going to be.

He thought about sneaking out early in the morning, but that would just make matters worse and there would be hell to pay when he came home at some point. He couldn't avoid it forever. But with the two asleep, Mourya figured that he could just be able to deal with it all in the morning. For the time being, he was going to tuck himself in for the night, leaving the two to have the couch for the evening.

The apartment remained quiet for several hours, with the exception of Mourya's snoring in the back room, but nothing seemed to disturb anyone from their slumber until the first sign of light. The obnoxious ring of Jane's cell phone went off, waking the man from sleep first. He was confused for a minute or so, wondering why he wasn't sleeping in his own bed until he saw Neha asleep and curled into his side. He had to admit that while he was confused, he was still quite thrilled that she was there.However, his cell phone demanded to be answered, and he swore the ringer was growing louder and louder with every passing second. Not wanting to risk Neha waking up so early, Jane carefully moved her so she would lie down before he grabbed his phone from the coffee table and walked out of the apartment.

Carefully closing the door behind him, he answered the call in a low voice.

"Hello?"

"Mr. Maya, this is..."

"Jane," he corrected the woman who spoke on the other line.

"Right Jane," the woman said, slightly irritated that he had taken the time to correct her when she had important matters to discuss. "My name is Daria, I'm calling from the office in regards to your mother,"

Jane swallowed before looking down at his feet, realising that he had fallen asleep with his shoes still on.

"Eh, right," he said, clearing his throat. "I heard that you would be calling."

"Mr. Jane, we've been trying to get into contact with you for quite some time, and when we have, you haven't been able to answer our questions pertaining to the arrangement of the funeral. Unfortunately, the doctors confirmed the death as an accidental overdose, caused by,"

"I don't need those particulars," Jane wiped his hands across his face."Really, I don't need those details."

What good was it going to do him to know how his mother died? What difference did it make that he hardly knew the woman as it was? He didn't know what she had been up to for over fifteen years, and she could have been dead during those times without him ever knowing. He was supposed to be feeling something about the situation now, but he wasn't sure what. Was he supposed to feel sad? Was it because Daria sounded so judgemental over the phone or the fact that he didn't want to know what his mother had overdosed on?

"We're assuming that you would want to make the funeral plans,"

He snapped. "And quite frankly, I do not want to make the funeral proceedings for a complete stranger. If you want to speak with my father, then call him and tell him to handle the situation! I don't want any involvement in this at all! Thank you for your time, Daria."

For a split second after he hung up the phone, Jane just wanted to throw his phone down the stairs and never answer a call again, but instead, he shoved the phone into his pocket before turning to enter the apartment again. Before he could, Mourya appeared in the doorway, gently closing the door behind him.

"Durde, what the hell is going on?" Mourya's voice was groggy; she never used to be awake so early in the morning. "Wake up to this and here you are yelling out, who the hell was on the phone?"

"From the office, telling me the cause of death and telling me that I have to attend the funeral proceedings. Didn't you tell me that you were talking to them and handling... "

"Well, I tried, but they were asking a lot of hard questions." Mourya told him. "I was going to talk to you about that..."

"When Mourya?" Jane's voice was still raised. "Before or after you tricked me into eating edibles?"

"Look, Jane..."

"No, Mourya, listen to me! You had no right to do that, not to me and certainly not to Neha. She has a job, and we have no idea if they do monthly drug screening. Just because your job doesn't do it doesn't mean that others follow the same protocol. You weren't thinking that they have to do a drug test. You think I'm going to get the job with that in my system?"

"But you two ate them,"

"We were upset and you put the chocolate in our faces. I would have to put an elephant's trunk in my mouth if it meant that it was going to calm me down. Neha had no idea what you were offering her... you don't think about these things! It must be great to be you... to live so carefree about everything, but a lot of us in this life can't do that! We can't be you! I can't be you! I can not waltz into a place and pick up any girl I want. You can do that, but I can't. I have to build up a relationship, be able to trust a person, and work at the pace of a snail in order to be comfortable. That's why I was internally freaking out yesterday when I asked Neha to move in with us. I didn't consult you, I just asked her, and that's not the type of person that I am. I 'I' I. "

Mourya had yet to utter a word, as Jane appeared to be completely losing it. He just stood in front of his best friend quietly, listening as if he were a child being scolded. Finally, Jane stopped and looked away from him, picking at the sleeves of his shirt to keep himself from pulling his own hair out.

"Jane," he finally spoke, smacking Jane's hand away from each other in order to get him to stop. "I'm sorry and I know I've told you this multiple times, but I'm sorry. I didn't mean to make matters worse. But you two were so upset and worked up last night that I didn't know what to do. I felt helpless that I couldn't get either one of you guys to chill out for a moment. It may not have been the best solution, but it was something and it got you to relax and sleep for a few hours. A few hours where you didn't have to worry about anything, and you can't deny that it's a nice feeling. "

"No, but..."

Jane went to argue, but the two men fell completely silent as they heard the sound of a loud thud come from inside the apartment.

"Neha?"

46

Things that Go Bump

The loud thud caused panic to strike Jane right in the chest, to the point where he suddenly felt his breathing become laboured just as he reached for the door. But he had to push through his own feelings at the time to make sure that Neha was alright. If she was suffering from a seizure due to the effects of the brownies hitting her system, he wasn't even sure where to begin, except with the plan of getting her to the hospital as fast as possible.

However, as he and Mourya barelled through the door, they found Neha herself on the floor, brushing herself off with an embarrassed look on her face. Her cheeks were a bright red and her gaze was averted to the floor as she didn't want to meet eyes with either of the men.

"Neha, are you alright?" Jane asked, rushing over. He didn't pick up on the clear signs that she was just fine physically.

"Y... yeah," she told him in a low voice. "Sorry, I just ended up tripping over the leg of the coffee table. I can be pretty clumsy sometimes, but I just felt a bit disoriented this morning and I wasn't paying attention to where I was stepping."

Jane sighed in relief. She didn't understand how happy he was that it hadn't been a seizure brought on by the special baked brownies, courtesy of Mourya. But he also wasn't sure how he was going to tell the girl that Mourya had not been fully honest about what had been in the treat he had offered to them the night before. He sincerely hoped that it would jeopardise her job because he wasn't sure if he could ever forgive Mourya for that one.

The man was known to do stupid things, but never to that extent and especially with someone with a medical condition. It was clear that Mourya had not been thinking at all when he offered the brownies. It could have easily caused harm to the woman, and then they all would have found themselves in an even bigger mess.

"Is everything alright?" Neha asked, noting the looks on the men's faces. "I did hear yelling out there. I wanted to make sure that nothing bad had happened out there."

Jane turned to Mourya with an expectant look, waiting for Mourya to confess his sins to Neha. Mourya gave him a pleading look as if he were a child about to self condemn for his crimes, but Jane showed no mercy while Neha remained looking back and forth between the two, looking highly confused. Finally, Mourya threw his head back and let out a loud sigh of defeat.

"Alright, alright, fine," he said, placing his hands up. "Okay, Neha, I made a mistake last night when I offered you those brownies. I, ugh, they were pot brownies... you know, edibles and I should have told you and.."

"I know what they were," Neha informed him.

The living room became silent as the men had their mouths open looking at her in shock. However, it only brought a smile to Neha's face.

"Well, come on now, Mourya, I figured it was a bit obvious," she said. "I know a pot brownie when I see one. I'm not a child. Although I do have to say, whoever made that batch went pretty strong with the oil."

Jane just stood with a blank expression while Mourya looked mighty pleased to be suddenly off the hook. He wasn't sure whether to be upset anymore, considering Neha didn't seem bothered by it in the slightest. But suddenly, she turned to him with a worried look.

"I hope this doesn't make you think ill of me, Jane," Neha said to him. "It's not something I regularly take part in. But it is something I have been researching because there are a lot of studies and claims that it really does help lessen seizures, to the point where people stop having them all together. I tried it once with a friend from work and it seemed to be alright, but I knew I could never get into it because I was living with Sasha and she would go absolutely mental if she thought I was taking part in something like that."

She really did look nervous in the moment, as she thought Jane was going to judge her for such a thing.

But Jane was only surprised to hear that it could possibly help with her seizures. It sounded like a great thing. He had heard some benefits of medical marijuana for some other conditions and illnesses, but he didn't even think of epilepsy.

"No, I don't think ill of you, Neha," he reassured her as she had been waiting for an answer. "I don't think I could ever think ill of you. I was just worried about the possibility of you losing your job or how it could harm you if you weren't aware. "

A smile appeared on her face before she walked over and kissed him on the cheek.

"You're incredibly sweet always, looking out for me in every way possible. But I promise you that it's fine. They don't do drug screenings at my job; just as long as we get the work done, that's all that matters."

"Well, that's good," Jane nodded her head, "then we don't have much to worry about, do we?"

He glanced over his shoulders at Mourya, wondering if he owed the man an apology, but Mourya shook his head. He knew he had been in the wrong to not disclose the information, but he was also thankful that it had all turned out well.

"Speaking of work," Neha said, "I do have to get myself dressed and head into the office for a bit if I actually want to keep my job."

"Go right ahead," Mourya told her."And don't rush; take all the time you need."

She offered another smile to the two before she left them alone in the living room. After a few moments had passed, Mourya turned to Jane.

"Dude, I am really sorry about all of this. I didn't mean it."

"No," Jane cut him off, "I guess this was a good thing after all. I could help her with the seizures, but she didn't want to do it. That must mean she feels comfortable around us to take part in it, right? "

"She's kissed you, worn your clothes, and is going to be moving in here, and you're questioning if she's comfortable with you. Jane, I swear to God... "

Mourya left Jane standing alone while shaking his head as Jane appeared confused for a few extra moments. He thought it was a valid question and it was a big difference for Neha to include them in such a big step. He didn't think taking such a substance would be a conversation that Neha would just share with anyone. It meant that she was comfortable with it, while she hadn't been comfortable in her sister's company. Jane didn't understand what Mourya had been getting at until about a minute later.

"Oh, right, I suppose she is comfortable around us then... oops. Hehe. "

47

Mistakes Were Made

After Neha left the apartment, Mourya decided to head out as well to grab some groceries before his work shift. Jane once again found himself alone in the apartment, and while he had always hated working under his father, he realised how much he missed work. He didn't miss the specific job, but he definitely missed keeping himself busy because when he was left alone with his thoughts, it wasn't the best time in the world. He knew he could start looking for work. But Jane was afraid to even put an application in because he was going to have to put down his previous employment and if they happened to call his father's company for a reference, he was probably never going to be hired again.

He was also feeling guilty for how he had spoken to the woman earlier, trying to deal with his mother's remains. However, Jane truly didn't know how to handle the situation. He hadn't seen the woman since she walked out of the home when he was just a boy. She didn't call, she didn't write, she didn't bother to check in on him at all. It was all because she was angry with Jane's father, and while it was understandable that she was upset with him, it was no excuse to abandon her son.

He grew up without a mother, but all of a sudden, nearly twenty years later, he was supposed to act as her son and provide for her? His father could not take responsibility for anything, especially his actions, and expected Jane to just do everything because Jane had to "man up."

Jane, furious with how everything was going on around him, settled his head onto the wooden table and sat in the silence of the apartment. There was the saving grace that he had Mourya in his life, and now he had Neha. Two incredible people who were willing to help him without him even asking. Yet, they came with their own stressors, Mourya often pushed him past the limits that Jane was comfortable with, and Jane worried like hell over Neha, especially with her family and Arjun constantly interfering.

In a perfect world, he would be able to live a happy and stress-free life with Neha and have Mourya there as usual. Neha's family and her epilepsy would be gone, so it wouldn't cause her stress, and they wouldn't even have to work; they would just be able to relax and be happy. That's all he wanted for the people he cared about... happiness.

Where things had gone wrong with his family, Jane wasn't sure, but it also didn't matter either because he couldn't go back in time to fix it. He had tried to mend ways with his father over the years, but it appeared as though it just wasn't meant to be. Jane was never going to be the person that his father wanted him to be, and his father was never going to be the person that Jane wanted him to be.

What a complicated mess Jane found himslef in.

Suddenly, there was a knock on the door, and he hesitated to stand up and answer it. Was it too much to ask to be left alone for the day? As the knocking persisted, it appeared so. He let out a frustrated groan before picking himself up from the table and walking over to the door. Without asking, he opened it up and found Arjun on the other side of the threshold. As soon as the door was open, Arjun's fist came straight for Jane's face, but Jane was fast with his reflexes, avoiding the incoming hit.

The man's fist went straight into the door as Jane tried to close it over, leaving the man to howl in pain.

"Arjun!" Sasha screeched. "I told you we weren't coming here to do that."

"What the hell are you doing here?" Jane asked, still trying to close the door over. "Get out of here before I call the police. You can't just come here and attack the people."

"No, wait!" Sasha called to him. "Jane, please, I swear I didn't come here for a fight, even if Arjun did. Please, I came to talk to Neha."

"She's not here and quite frankly, Sasha, I don't think she's in any mood to talk to you! Not after the behaviour of you two yesterday. She was extremely upset and cried.

"I know! I know! We were stupid," Sasha claimed, her voice full of desperation as she seemed to want to talk to her sister and perhaps apologize. "I just... I need her to come here, Jane. She needs to be home where people can be there to take care of her."

Jane shook his head. "You didn't understand anything she said yesterday, you didn't grasp any of it. She doesn't want people to take care of her; she wants people to respect her as a person. She may have a condition, but she is not a child. She is an adult and she has a handle on her condition to the best of her ability at this point in time. Perhaps things will get better for her without being surrounded by the stress that you keep adding onto her."

"Jane, you don't understand. She thought she could be independent, and that ended up with her driving her car straight into a tree. She had a seizure on the train because she refused to have people drive her. She's too stubborn for her own good. You don't know her like I do."

"You're right," Jane said quietly. "I know her better than you do, apparently, and that's a damn shame on your behalf."

"You can't take care of her!" Arjun said trying to push open the door again, "she needs a man to be there."

"Then you certainly shouldn't be suggesting it yourself," Jane said. "I may not be a manly man, but I'm a gentleman and I'm proud to be one. If you two don't leave, I will have no problem calling the police. If Neha wishes to contact you, she will do it on her own terms, not on the terms of being harassed. "

It appeared as though they wanted to protest, but with Jane threatening to call the police if they didn't leave, they turned to go. As soon as he was able to close the door over again without Arjun pushing against it, Jane locked it as fast as he possibly could. He pressed himself against it and shook his head in disbelief at the scenario that had just unfolded. Just as he went to move back to his seat, more frantic knocking came from the door.

"Jane! Jane!" He heard Sasha's voice calling to her, bringing him to roll his eyes.

"You need to leave..."

"Jane, Neha is in the hospital!"

He didn't think Sasha would be one to lie about such matters. Why she was telling him, he wasn't sure. He assured her that she wouldn't want to tell him because it would leave her to deal with Neha all by herself, but as he opened the door and saw the woman in tears, he knew that it wasn't some sort of sick prank.

"She was with you. Did she say that she wasn't feeling well this morning before she went to work?" Sasha asked as he led her down the stairs towards her car after closing the door behind him. "She normally gets a bad feeling before a big one happens. Did she say anything?"

"No," Jane shook his head, "She was fine this morning. She was in a good mood and she said, "Oh no..."

48

420, What's Your Emergency?

Jane would never have imagined that he would find himself stuck in a vehicle with Sasha and Arjun, especially after the scene that had taken place in his apartment just prior to Sasha getting the phone call from the hospital. He was terribly uncomfortable just being around them, let alone trapped in the same car with them, but he didn't say anything. Instead, he was trying to focus on a loose thread on his shirt to keep himself distracted. Once again, his mind drifted to the pot brownies that Neha had consumed in the recent hours, and he thought of her going off her specific diet as the doctors had directed her. He wondered if his influence and Mourya's mistake had caused a major reaction despite what Neha had said about marijuana being helpful for her seizures.

Sasha was trying to come up with answers. As usual, Neha exhibited sighs before a bad one, but she was drawing blanks. She proceeded to blame herself for adding to Neha's stress, which never helped the situation to begin with. Jane thought about telling Sasha about Neha's change in diet, but he figured he would hold off. There was no sense in confessing it at the moment, as it would only get her and Arjun worked up, and he could possibly get out of the car. He was also sure that the doctors were probably already aware of it in Neha's system. If Neha had already come to her conscious state, then she probably already confessed.

He was just going to have to see what the situation was like when they arrived at the hospital. Arjun had yet to say a word to Jane after he encountered and stood off, keeping himself busy by paying attention to the road quietly. However, every so often, the two men made eye contact through the rear view mirror. Jane would have felt bad for Arjun.

When they arrived at the hospital, the adults climbed out of the car. Arjun didn't give two galances at the state of his terrible parking job as they rushed inside to find someone who would be able to tell them where Neha was and what happened. According to the nurse at the rounded desk, Neha wasn't in as bad of condition as Sasha made it sound. She did take a rather nasty fall as the seizure had a sudden onset while she was walking on the sidewalk on the way to her work building. Unfortunately, she had fallen before she could attempt to lower herself down, leaving her to scrape her chin and jawline against the sidewalk and hit her head.

Luckily, people rushing towards other buildings for work or other reasons had stopped to assist the girl, one of them calling 108 to get her the help she needed. But she was awake in her room, talking to the doctor about her medication and alternatives that she was hoping to switch to.

"Switch medications?" Sasha immediately shook her head. "If she's fallen, I don't think she's in the right mindset to be making such decisions. That's something that my mother and I should be discussing with her.

"I'm going to have to disagree with you there," Jane said before the nurse could intervene, "at last I checked, Neha is an adult and you're not a doctor. If a doctor believes she is coherent enough to make her own decisions, then he would be more qualified to say what she's able to do than you. "

Oh, how Jane hated Sasha and Arjun because whenever he disagreed with them, they looked as though they would chew off his head right there to defend himself. It wouldn't be fair for them to try and call all the shots. Her autonomy had not been lost when she was diagnosed with epilepsy; she was competent to make her own decisions about her body and what medications she wanted to take.

Not saying another word, Jane looked down at his shoes until he was quiet, waiting for the nurse to continue. However, before she could speak, the doctor arrived, introducing herself.

"Hello," the woman says, her wrinkles near her eyes creasing as she looks at them all with a friendly expression."Which one of you is Jane?"

Sasha and Arjun were lighting Jane on fire a million times with their looks in his direction, as Jane seemed surprised by the sudden request.

"Er... that's me," he said, raising his hands as if he were in elementary school again.

"Ah, Neha wanted to speak with you personally while I talked to her sister," she turned to Sasha, "I'm assuming you are Sasha?"

"Yes, ma'am," Sasha nodded her head. "But I think I should be the one to talk to Neha."

"Unfortunately, that was not the request at the moment, and I'd really like to keep her as comfortable as possible."

While Jane didn't want to stir any more trouble into the pot between him and the other two adults, he was anxious to see Neha and how she was doing. His fingers were nearly ripping at his sweater as he continued to pull at the hem to calm himself. The doctor directed him towards the room while she remained behind with Sasha. As he created some distance between him and the group, Jane felt a little better, but his breathing still felt quite restricted as he wasn't sure what he was going to see when he saw Neha.

But when he walked into the assigned room, he wasn't expecting to find her sitting in the room with a white sheet over her head.

"Uh, Neha?" he called out to her. She looked like a child attempting to be a ghost, leaving him bewildered.

"Hey, Jane," she said in a low voice.

"Any particular reason as to why you are under the covers?"

"Because my face is hideous right now. I blushed it all up when I fell, and I feel really stupid."

"You feel stupid because you fell, but it wasn't your fault, and I know you don't look hideous right now, but that's physically impossible, you know." He said, making his way to the bed and sitting down.

"Yeah, you're just saying that to make me feel better. But you haven't seen this car wreck right now."

Slowly, he reached out his hand and pulled the sheet to reveal her face. As it was stated, she really did bang up her chin and jaw from the fall, scraping it and bruising the sides, but it wasn't as bad as she thought it was. She was probably just being too hard on herself and feeling embarrassed about not being able to sense the seizure before it came on.

"Neha, what happened? Was it... the stuff? "

The way he tried to reference the weed brownies made Neha laugh before she met his gaze.

"Unfortunately," she sighed.

"But I thought you said it was good for people with epilepsy. It's meant to help."

"And it is and it does, Jane. But there's a difference between weed and cannabis oil being used.The THC is the difference between how it interacts with my medication. Apparently, it might be getting to the point where my seizures are becoming medication resistant, and for people like that, doctors have been looking into medical marijuana as a treatment, but it's way different from the stuff that you buy off the guy on the street, you know? It had a bad reaction when I took my medication this morning before work, and you can't even be sure that the stuff you buy off the street is even 'kosher', if you catch my drift. Sometimes it can be laced with other stuff..."

Jane looked mortified.

"Neha, I'm so sorry, I know Mourya does..."

"Jane, it's fine really. I'm actually glad this happened in some way. I've been waiting for the opportunity to bring it up with my doctor, but I never saw the perfect time because Sasha or my mother were always around and they never let me make decisions for myself. But this was kind of the perfect opportunity presenting itself in disguise. "

"I'm not sure what's perfect about you getting hurt in order to bring up a decision with your doctor..." he frowned.

"I'm not exactly thrilled about smashing my face into the pavement either, but I'm happy that I can freely discuss another possible treatment. I can be off that stupid diet. I can be off all those medications that didn't work. This might be the start of some really big changes. The doctor was talking about some patients that started on medical cannabis using the indica strain stuff and they haven't had seizures in over a year. Maybe this is exactly what I needed. "

49

The 'M' Word

Neha was glad that she had told the doctor to let Jane in first so she could talk to him and relax, rather than have to deal with her sister freaking out. However, as time went on, she knew she was going to have to face Sasha and tell her what really happened, and she was going to have to face her mother.

"I know what you're thinking," Jane said to her in a quiet voice, "and you don't have to see anyone until you're ready to do so. No one is going to force you to see anyone if you don't want to."

She leaned back on her pillow and nodded her head. "I know, I wish I could just see you and be down for the day, but that's not fair to them. As much as Sasha drives me up the wall, along with my mother, I can't ignore everything they've done for me since I was a little girl. I know they annoy me to hell some days, but I know they do it because they care. "

"I understand they care, Neha," Jane said, leaning forward on the bed, "but caring doesn't make it right for what they say or do to you.They may think they are doing the right thing, but if no one corrects them, they are going to keep it. They may have sacrificed a lot for you, and it's an amazing thing what humans will do, but do not forget the sacrifice you have made to ensure they stay happy as well."

"I wish it were as simple as just saying that to them and having them understand," Neha replied as she went to pull the blanket over her head again. Her body was aching terribly from her fall, as the seizure gave her no warning to sit down to avoid the impact of the pavement. Her face certainly hurt like hell. As much as she wanted to lift her hand and touch it, she was given a painful reminder at every attempt to do so.

"I'm sure, given the circumstances and having the doctor talk to them, your mother and sister will understand that you have different needs and wants right now. It's something they cannot provide, and if they truly cared, they would be willing as before to do whatever it takes to help you feel better. Even if it includes keeping their mouths shut and letting you make the decisions. "

Hidden by the blanket, Jane couldn't see the smile on Neha's face, but she was practically grinning ear to ear. The way he spoke so confidently and with such power in his voice, it was so much different from the man that could barely utter a hello aboard the train. When she learned that he had gotten into the same car with Sasha and Arjun, he suddenly became the bravest person in the entire world in her eyes. After all, the horrible and nasty things that were said to him, the threats made, Jane put all of that aside to be there for her. If that didn't speak volumes to those around them that questioned the relationship, Neha didn't care because she knew exactly what type of person Jane was.

perfect in an imperfect way.

The blanket was suddenly pulled down by her own hand, bringing Jane to look over at her with a curious glance. But he wasn't given much of a chance to question what she was doing until he found himself locked in a kiss with her. It made him nervous, but at the same time, he was incredibly giddy on the inside.

When she pulled away, he needed a moment to collect himself as he swallowed and sat in a daze for a moment.

"What was that for?" He finally managed to ask. It's not the typical question to ask after sharing a passionate kiss, but it made Neha laugh.

The man turned red in the face before he shook his head. He wouldn't describe himself as wonderful ever before, but to hear Neha describe him as such, he felt some weight lifted off his shoulders. All his life, he had been hoping that someone besides Mourya would look at him and see some sort of potential. The potential to be a friend, a boy friend, a possible husband, or just an equal. After all, he was human. Even though he did have his quirks, it didn't make him less human as many others thought. To hear the woman that he admired so much describe him as wonderful and willing to kiss him in public was a giant step in the right direction.

If others could see him as wonderful and love him, then he could start to see it for himself and love himself as well. He was speechless, but it was a good thing as he took Neha's hands and just held onto them tightly.

It seemed to be a perfect moment, one out of a Hallmark movie, but they weren't being directed by a movie crew and the end scene wouldn't be perfect as the hospital door burst open and Neha's mother had arrived.

Jane was frozen in place under the intimidating glare of the matriarch, while Neha looked close to just running and jumping out of the nearest window.

"Really, Neha? Really? " Her mother stomped over to where her daughter was in bed. "At first, I thought you'd gone insane when you started dating a new one, but now... he's got you... smoking the... marijuana?"

"Mom..."

"And you?" her mother turned to Jane. "You're trying to corrupt my daughter. You are forcing her to do all of these horrible things.

Jane's eyes widened to the point where he nearly thought they were going to pop out of his eye sockets when her mother was suddenly struck back with a pillow. Neha had thrown the pillow to get the woman attacking Jane, and everyone in the room seemed surprised by her actions, including Neha.

"Did you... did you just throw a pillow at me?" she asked her daughter.

"Yes," Neha answered, "I did, and I have more as ammo. Don't you dare try to go after Jane like that again. Also, I didn't smoke marijuana, I ingested some edibles, and before you go on the rant that drugs are bad, think about all the hell I've been putting in my body since I received the diagnosis. I've been on stronger drugs with a prescription before I was a teenager. "

"Those aren't illegal drugs; they were prescribed to help you."

"And CBD oil has been helping others in the states where it's been legalized, and New York is one of them. The doctor is going to sign me up for a trial. They've already been doing trials with children with Epidiolex. It's supposed to be helping those where the medication is no longer helping. "

"Well, if this weed oil is as good as you say it is, then why is it only being brought up now?" She placed her hands on her hips.

"Because I knew this is how you were going to react, just like Sasha did."

"You were on a diet..."

"It wasn't working!" Jane spoke now, looking directly at the woman. Neha had her hand in place over a pillow just in case. "The only thing the diet was doing was making your daughter miserable, and the medication wasn't doing its job. She needs something else and the doctors are trying to help. Why are you so against this?"

"My daughter is not going to be some pothead..."

"You're absolutely correct," Jane interrupted, "she's not going to be a pothead, she's going to be happy and hopefully seizure-free." The doctor said that it could increase her appetite as well, which would help her gain the weight that she wanted to. She's not smoking weed. Doctors wouldn't allow her to run around with a blunt in hand. And for your information, I don't smoke or anything of the sort, but I fully support Neha during this time and you should too. You are her mother, after all. She needs you and Sasha to be as supportive as possible. Don't make the mistakes that my mother made of abandoning her child when they needed her the most. "

50

Trial and Error

While Neha liked to think of her seizure as a blessing in disguise, Jane wished it hadn't come down to such a terrifying moment for the woman to finally get the message through to her mother and sister. Arjun was a lost cause altogether, and he wasn't healthy for Neha. With him hopefully out of the picture, as Neha had refused to let him into the hospital room, Jane could only hope that she was closing that chapter in her life and opening a new one.

Neha needed alternate treatment, but it wasn't just in medication form. She needed better treatment when it came to her mother and Sasha. They needed to listen to Neha and her wants and needs, not what they just assumed would be best for her. Perhaps because they were older and didn't have a disorder, they automatically assumed that they were what was best for Neha, but it wasn't the case at all. After allowing them to dictate her life in hopes of keeping them happy, Neha was finally free to do what she needed for herself, and Jane couldn't be any happier for her.

Jane had started the clinical trials on the CBD oils to see if it would reduce her seizures. She had hoped that everything was going to work out fine for her. She was strong physically and mentally, exactly what she needed to get through the new changes. While he had been the one to scold Mourya earlier for introducing Neha to the edibles, it seemed the man was due for an apology. After all, if it hadn't been for him, they wouldn't have found themselves in the situation to begin with. If only it didn't involve Neha suffering a seizure and smashing her head against the pavement, that would have been a lot better in Jane's head.

But as the man left the hospital to collect some clothing from the apartment for Neha, he had a smile on his face as he boarded one of the town's buses. Sasha had offered to give him a ride back but he politely declined, although he was pretty sure that Neha probably would have liked to get her sister out of the room as soon as possible.

Sasha and her mother weren't exactly thrilled to hear about the cannabis oil trials, but with the hope of it helping Neha, they couldn't really argue. They were just going to have to accept the fact that they no longer had control of the situation. It fell into Neha's hands, where it rightfully belonged.

For Neha to only welcome him into the hospital room above anyone else, it finally clicked in Jane's mind that he didn't give himself enough credit. Neha didn't want her sister, her mother, Arjun, or even anyone with her in the room. She wanted him. She was confined to him and trusted him. It meant the world to Jane as the realisation settled in. For the man who couldn't even think of uttering the word "hello" to the woman months ago, he was now the one she called upon when she needed someone the most.

His mother didn't need Jane.

His father didn't need Jane.

But Neha wanted and needed Jane, and that was all that mattered to him because it was all he wanted and needed.

During the time of the trials, Jane would be there for Neha in any way that she needed, whether she wasn't feeling the greatest or if she suddenly found herself starving in the middle of the night and needed to get food. If she decided that the CBD oil was not for her, he would be there to support her and help her find something to help. He would spend the rest of his life looking up alternate treatments for Neha as long as they helped her. Because people like Neha didn't deserve to suffer, they deserved a lifelong period of happiness.

Arriving at the apartment, Jane noticed that Mourya was not home as he went to dig for his key in his pocket. He would call the man and leave a message, and then probably leave a note inside the apartment for added measure. Just as he went to open the door, he heard a throat clear down that led up to the door, causing him to jump. Jane looked to see his father making his way up the stairs.

For a moment, the young man couldn't breathe, wondering if he had accidentally fallen asleep on the bus and was trapped in a dream. There was no reason for his father to be there; not even the death of his mother had brought so much as a phone call from the man. Yet, as Jane pinched himself repeatedly and didn't wake up, he realised that it was real; his father approaching him was happening in real life.

Jane was going to question how his father knew where he lived, but it clicked that he had worked for his father and there was bound to be something with his address on it. of the fact that his father could get anything he wanted just by calling on one of his little busy bodies to do the work for him.

"Wh... what..." Jane began stammering, unable to look his father in the eye right away. However, he squeezed his fists down by his side and took a deep breath. If he was able to stand up to Arjun, Sasha, and her mother, he could stand up to his father too.

"What are you doing here?" Jane asked in a quiet voice.

Jane only stared at him, not daring to say a word, but completely disgusted by his father's tone. There was no remorse, no sadness that he had approached his son about his ex-wife's death so casually as if they were exchanging something.

When Jane didn't say anything, Mr. Krishnan suddenly began to feel awkward as he stood on the top step. Maybe he was waiting for Jane to get emotional, for Jane to apologize, for Jane to at least react, but instead, his son continued to stare at him in silence.

"In the wake of your mother's death," Mr. Krishnan continued, "I can offer you your job back. Just as long as you show up on time and do as you are told from now on. "

"No!" Jane snapped, shaking his head from left to right. "I'm sorry, sir, but I believe you have the wrong apartment. I don't have a mother and a father. They died when I was just a boy. I'd also like to work at a place where I'd be respected and not ridiculed under a dictatorship. Now, if you would excuse me, there's a cute soul that is waiting for me to return. The same one that I lost my job over by trying to help her. Funny how things work out, right?"

With a turn of the doorknob, Jane opened the door to his apartment and walked in without another word to him. He closed the door swiftly and stood inside his apartment for a few moments, trying to figure out if he had actually just stood up to his father for the final time.

"I did it. I actually did it. "

What a relief it would be to finally have all the weight off his shoulders that he had been carrying for so long against his will. Finally, he could breathe and there was plenty of fresh air around him.

Epilogue

Mourya hurried through the cold night air on his way up to the apartment. The winter breeze was not being kind to anyone that evening. His ears felt as though they were about to fall off, and the alcohol in his system was not even helping to warm him up. It was his own fault for drinking, knowing damn well he could have driven, but some things never change for Mourya. Nights were full of strange girls, drinking and regrets in the morning, just how he liked it. However, that night, he was going to take some time off from his routine as he had other plans.

A skip up the steps, the man knocked on the door before putting his hands over his mouth and trying to warm them with his own breath. He could hear the sound of rummaging behind the door, causing his body to become frenzied with anticipation.

"Come on, Jane, I'm freezing off out here!" "Open the door, man!"

The sound of the lock turning clicked before the door opened, revealing Jane on the other side. Before the man could say anything, Mourya bulldozed his way inside.

"Oh God, it's cold out here! Were you trying to get me to turn into frost? "

"Mourya, you have a key. Where is it?" Jane asked, placing his hands on his hips.

The two men stared at each other with stern expressions before they broke into grins and pulled each other into a hug.

"Happy Christmas, my friend; well, Christmas Eve, but you get the point," Mourya told him. "It feels like it's been ages since I've seen you, even though that hasn't been the case at all. But how have you been adjusting to the new place and getting settled in? "

"It's been good," Jane nodded as they pulled away from the hug, "There's a lot more room than the last place, which was definitely needed, you know? And the neighbourhood is nice, which is a plus... and we're further away from Neha's family. "

"Always a boon," Mourya chuckled, "but where is the lady of the house?" in the back resting, or..."

"No, she went out to drop some gifts at her mother's house and spend a little time there, but she should be back any minute."

"Look at her, driving by herself again. It's amazing. It's been what... two years now since she started on the CBD? Not even one seizure in sight."

"Two and a half, but who's counting?" Jane smiled. "But yeah, she worked up the courage to get back into it and the doctors said she was free to do so. Technically, she only had to wait a year before she could get her licence back, but hey, it didn't hurt to wait either. We've had plenty to keep us busy in the meantime."

Neha walked in, surprised to see Mourya arrive so late in the evening.

"What's going on?" she asked with a small laugh. "Mourya, we weren't expecting you until tomorrow."

"I know, but I texted Jane earlier and told him that I was in the neighborhood, so here I am. You got me a day earlier, Neha. Merry Christmas. "

She walked over and embraced the man in a tight hug. "It's good to see you. I'm glad you could make it."

"Does she still blame it on weed?" Mourya asked in a teasing voice.

"She blames everything on it. Well, that and the democratic party, but we don't get into that discussion," Neha smiled before looking over.

"AND IT ALL STARTED WITH THAT LETTER, QUEEN JANE, AND IT'S NOWHERE NEAR OVER."

About the Author

Author Sateesh Patil, known for his debut - HOW JANE MET NEHA RAJ, is a English Romantic writer, researcher and philosopher. He is know for romanticizing the feminine and nature in his writings, has established various fund raisers and contributing victims effected by epilepsy and mental health related issues. Descent of Royal Maratha family and reigning as a social influencer and reviewer from Hyderabad-India.

www.ingramcontent.com/pod-product-compliance
Lightning Source LLC
La Vergne TN
LVHW041013150826
845672LV00001B/74

* 9 7 9 8 8 4 7 6 7 8 3 3 9 *